Mean Bastards
Making Nice

Critical Praise for the books of Djelloul Marbrook

Artemisia's Wolf

...successfully blends humor and satire (and perhaps even a touch of magic realism) into its short length ...an engrossing story, but what might strike the reader most throughout the book is its infusion of breathtaking poetry...a stunning rebuke to notoriously misogynist subcultures like the New York art scene, showing us just how hard it is for a young woman to be judged on her creative talent alone.

—Tommy Zurhellen, *Hudson River Valley Review*

Saraceno

...Djelloul Marbrook writes dialogue that not only entertains with an intoxicating clickety-clack, but also packs a truth about low-life mob culture "The Sopranos" only hints at. You can practically smell the anisette and filling-station coffee.

—Dan Baum, author of *Gun Guys* (2013) and *Nine Lives: Mystery, Magic, Death and Life in New Orleans* (2009) and others

...a good ear for crackling dialogue ... I love Marbrook's crude, raw music of the streets. The notes are authentic and on target ...

—Sam Coale, *The Providence (RI) Journal*

...an entirely new variety of gangster tale ... a Mafia story sculpted with the most refined of sensibilities from the clay of high art and philosophy ... the kind of writer I take real pleasure in discovering ...a mature artist whose rich body of work is finally coming to light."

—Brent Robison, editor, *Prima Materia*

Far from Algiers

...as succinct as most stanzas by Dickinson... an unusually mature, confidently composed first poetry collection.

—Suzanna Roxman, *Prairie Schooner*

...brings together the energy of a young poet with the wisdom of long experience.

—Edward Hirsch, Guggenheim Foundation

Brushstrokes and Glances

Whether it is commentary on state power, corporate greed, or the intensely personal death of a loved one, Djelloul Marbrook is clear sighted, eloquent, and precise. As the title of the collection suggests, he uses the lightest touch, a collection of fragments, brushstrokes and glances, to fashion poems that resonate with truth and honesty.

—Phil Constable, *New York Journal of Books*

Mean Bastards Making Nice

Two Novellas

Djelloul Marbrook

LEAKY BOOT PRESS

Mean Bastards Making Nice—Two Novellas
by Djelloul Marbrook

First published in 2014 by
Leaky Boot Press
http://www.leakyboot.com

ISBN: 978-1-909849-12-9

Contents

Book 1

The Pain of Wearing Our Faces

in memory of
Artemis and Hecate

A work of art has an author and yet,
when it is perfect, it has something
which is anonymous about it.

—Simone Weill

I don't trust words. That's what he said. They're swindlers, mean bastards making nice, he said.

I felt like swatting his words out of my head as I swarmed into Bloomie's on Christmas Eve in full city roast. I needed gloves. I needed a new head. I'd left my rabbit-lined Danish gloves in a cab. The cheap wool mark-ups I bought made my two first-water rubies and clitoral opal itch. You don't want to itch anywhere, but in Bloomie's razzle of cut-glass perfume pumps and dazzle of capitalist excess itching is a criminal impulse. I gulped three Benadryl caplets with my own spit.

On a good day my sexual jewels are eyes for seeing in the dark, sensors to explore ocean floors, microscopes. On a bad day, they're nails to bleed me on a cross, tear me apart. Today they itch and shine at trouble up ahead, like all good jewels. Isn't it what they're for? I'm an artist. I never know trouble in my head, it's always somewhere else, tactile, fragrant, unwilling, unable to be put off. Why else would a woman want to be an artist? Trouble comes with paint, out of tubes, luxuriant, much too rich. You can cut it, but only to make it mobile and subtler. How would an artist paint without these sensational jewels? You'd have to ask a man. Lots of luck with that. If you ask me—I know you didn't—Adam's a throwback and human institutions exist to distract us from that truth. I'm sure he has his uses, but finding one only occasionally appeals to my imagination.

You might just enjoy this little story if you keep in mind I take nothing seriously that I can't paint.

***

Christmas is the loneliest day, even in the midst of family. Despite our efforts to celebrate a birth, it's funereal. Everyone tries to make it so perfect they wind up reminding themselves they're going to die. Gift-wrapped, of course. The buildings dumped slush on me as I headed towards Saint Thomas Church on Fifth Avenue. In the wet gloaming to the rear of the great nave I sat behind a famous English actor and his family, sweating rivulets down to my pubes. The candles looked like globs of swamp gas.

I looked around for mean bastards, then I remembered my friend—well, friend, for lack of a better word—had meant words. Words were his mean bastards. Being an artist, I thought that amusing. I'm always prepared to think the worst of words, especially about art. I remembered a big banner over a Nam June Paik exhibition at the Corcoran in Washington, DC, claiming *Print Is Dead*. Yes, words are mean bastards, any artist can tell you. I chuckled like a crazy lady. I am a crazy lady.

The three priests at the altar, their backs turned to us, expressing religion's perfect contempt, leaned in unison to the left, then to the right, reminding me of a shadowy Max Schreck playing Nosferatu. Three Nosferatus. My next chuckle nabbed the actor's attention. I would have liked to share this vagrant whimsy with him. He smiled as if he'd read my mind. But he struck me as the kind of guy who'd smile at street ladies, too.

***

The priest refused eye contact at the altar rail and hurt my front tooth as he clutched the chalice. I needed a real drink. So I went to one of my AA meetings that evening in the parish hall of Calvary Saint George. The hall was a fug of burnt coffee, retting wool, cigarette redolence and viral spew. I stood in the ogee arch and barfed a loathsome grenade that just missed someone's coattail. I thought of a herald angel retching and laughed bitterly. My camel-haired target turned and looked stricken. I didn't belong there. I didn't belong back at the class I taught at Cooper Union, the one where The Heron told me he didn't trust words. He used them pretty damned well for a man who didn't trust them. I didn't trust him. Brush strokes maybe he trusted, he said. Musical notes. It made me seasick, all his finicking to say the right thing. I think he's one of those people who are at pains to know just what you want them to say. There are paintings like that, too many in fact.

I left the parish hall suppressing an impulse to cackle. Every thought that came into my head tasted like vomit. It was one of those days when your past grabs your hair and tosses you into traffic. I keep trying to paint a picture of me flying about twelve feet high over a sidewalk. Some kind of squall is pursuing me, and I can't get up higher out of its reach. I'm not good enough to paint this dream.

I don't feel the way I look. A lot of trouble starts right there. I know the damned pain of wearing an unbelonging face. Mine looks as if it's being worn by a seven-foot Viking who has just clambered out of a dragon ship on the East Anglia coast with unholy mayhem in mind. It makes people blanch. It's austere and you'd have to've had a bent childhood to get the hots for it. But some men and women do. I want to torture their mothers. I'm tall, almost as tall as that suspect inveigher against words in my class, and I tend to slip through crowds and in and out of places like a shiv of light. You might think I'm ahead of you full-on, but then I turn sideways into a sheet of glass and am gone.

My students like me because there's no blather in me. I just put my hand on theirs and teach them how to paint. I don't care how they paint, I just want them to enjoy it. My students use more paint than any other class. They leave my class looking guilty, because they're having fun. So why did this word-baiter want to impress me? He'd heard me start the semester saying, You can talk, I don't talk, I paint, so I hope that's what you're here for. I saw his face toting me up like a bill. When he casually, too casually, remarked to his part of the room that he didn't trust words I felt like painting on his back. I get these whims. I think I drink to suppress them. One evening not long after that I just started painting on his white shirt. The students behind me nudged each other. He just kept on painting as I stooped behind him painting his mournful face on his back. As the clock ran out on us the students gathered around me in silence. He stood, took off his shirt, hung it over a canvas and studied it.

When he was finished he looked me in the eye and nodded. My face bunched around my eyes as the students poked each other. That'll teach him to bandy words with me, I thought.

***

I was wiping off a damp Washington Square bench with one hand and holding a cup of coffee in the other a month later when one my students stopped to ask me if I knew who my victim was. No, I said. A famous composer, teaches at Juilliard, the student said. A few weeks after that I learned that the shirt I'd desecrated was a six-hundred-dollar Albini Egyptian cotton custom-made in Milan.

The Heron had no sense of color, but he was becoming a good draftsman. I told him to carry a small pad and look for detail, not a face but a mouth, not a facade but a cornice. Do mouths, I told him, then you can do anything. Look at Daumier. The Heron reacted like a crazed assassin receiving orders. You have to be a kind of terrorist to draw well.

Then one night I saw him in the Broome Street Spice Cafe with his pad in front of him. He looked up and nodded. I thought of the Albini shirt and walked over to him. An apology was due, but I wasn't in the mood. Look, I said, I can smell craziness out of the tube, like one color from another. Then I waited for a question, ready to hate any question. If he just nods again, I thought, I'm going to fetch my coffee and spill it on him.

I'm drawn to terrorists, he said.

There he was again, picking thoughts out of my head.

I look in the mirror, he said, and I say, Hey, look at me, I'm terrified, I must be alive. When the proof seems insufficient I start drinking. It's like shocking a sick well with chlorine.

When people are plucking interesting thoughts out of their heads they tend to peel the walls with their eyes. Or they look like they're studying someone behind you. But The Heron looked like he'd found his own reflection in my pupils. I felt something almost like love for this. I thought he probably wrote good music. I paint like that. Alert for the slightest imperfection that might improve the work. It could be a streak caused by debris at the

16

mouth of the tube. It could be a waver around some mote in the paper. Sometimes the beauty of the eye is in the tic.

He didn't invite me to sit down. I didn't ask. I had a sense he liked me standing there, like a note well struck.

I'm a drunk too, I said, my legs spread belligerently. I'd be at a meeting right now, but sometimes they depress me. It depresses me I need them. They're like coloring books. I can't fill them in. Nobody can. Some days I'd rather get mugged. Other days I just sit there and let the testimonies wash over me. It's like bathing in my own compassion.

He put a fork down, caught the waiter's eye and scribbled in the air. I put some money on my own table and we left together.

I don't write for anyone under thirty—they're all deaf, he told me. Restaurants give me an earache. We have a deafening society because we're afraid to be alone with ourselves. I don't know how we can think straight with all the white noise, he said.

Yes, a deaf and pixeled society too, I offered cheerily. Had I meant pixilated? I didn't know. Artists don't have to know. I kicked my legs out as I do when I'm trying to walk something off. That's hard to do during the day, too many people. He savored my shins flashing under the street lights and then peered over at me as if he'd tasted something good. He skipped twice to fall into step with me, and then, spectral and attuned, we walked on in silence.

What kind of terrorists?

Women mostly. Like my mother. You never know what they're going to do, but you can count on it to be ugly.

That's how you feel about women?

It's how I feel about the ones I'm drawn to.

I let go a measured woof and he laughed.

Well, I guess you don't have to worry about me, I said. And I don't have to worry about you.

Oh, I knew that when you painted my face. It wasn't at all like tormenting the one you're attracted to. No, it was like getting up in the middle of the night to make a notation or to paint something. If you don't do it, you're not serious. I knew that. It was a great privilege. I matted the shirt, you know, and framed it under glass, yes. It's—he swallowed—it's me all right, and I'm not looking too anxious to know me. I'll have to make the effort if I stay sober. Otherwise all bets are off, right? I mean, what good's it being sober if you're still fourteen years old?

Yeah, well, fourteen was a bad year. I dunno, I didn't have any good years until I made my first good painting. Then I thought, Okay, that's why you're here, to make one more good painting. Fact is, that's how I started sobering up. I saw a Parmigianino drawing in The Frick, and I thought, Jesus, this happened in this world, so maybe it's worth inhabiting after all. I mean, who can imagine a human being like that? It's easier for me to imagine Jesus.

* * *

The Heron kept coming to class. I didn't know whether he'd fixated on anything about me. I like to know such things. For me, it was his eyes. His green irises were rimmed in brown; elongated golden spheroids radiated from the pupils at intervals. They were extraordinarily still. I kept encouraging him to draw. I urged him to spend time at The Drawing Center on Wooster Street. I thought paint would sidetrack him. He was a composer, so he knew about being seduced. He had a micro-vision that amused me. For example, he sketched a doorway in the West Village with great precision, but when you looked closely you saw that it was beginning to melt. I thought of the two of us as nut jobs playing strip poker under an institutional stairwell and I could hardly look at him. That's why I drink, by the way, because men make strange under my nose. Men making strange is a phrase in an Anglican hymn. When I first heard it I thought I'd faint for the exquisiteness of it. It affirmed something I couldn't describe. People making strange is why parties are like Pauline's worst peril to me. I'm tied to the tracks and faces bear down on me like freight trains. I understand the world like an electrician. It's filled with uncapped hot wires, scorched junction boxes, frayed wires, jury-rigged circuitry, overloads and sizzling grids. What I touch is hot and loose. Saboteurs throw breakers in moldy cellars. Fuses blow in secret places. Uncoded wires cross unaccountably. I glance at someone and I see their secret face and I can't ever look at them equably again. Your face is at risk in my eyes, and you know it. I start making collages in my head. The collages spin and rush me. I drink to slow them down. I can't stand parties or meetings. Every image pelts me. I have no filters. That's why I drink. That's why I paint.

These faces... a therapist would say, touching his fingertips. I'd jump up and shout Fuck you, they're mine, my truths, not one of them has ever lied to me. When I see someone wearing a second face I see what that person doesn't want me to see. I know all about schizophrenia, its tuning by Torquemada. I wouldn't trade it away any more than a manic-depressive would trade her gorgeous mania. But I'd like to enjoy it without the toll booze exacts. I'd like to get away with it, which is why I kept on thinking about The Heron, because he was trying to get away with something too. We were both trying to pull off something taboo. We're always at war with what we need. We didn't need each other, not as two urgent bodies wobbling in unstable orbits. Not that way. But each of us had something the other needed, or maybe we were the only trustworthy repositories we could find. I didn't necessarily trust somebody I paid to sit and listen to me making the sign of the phallus with his fingertips, and while the AA was helping me stay sober I was thirty-nine going on nineteen at best.

* * *

Then one night he buzzed up from the street. I shot a sable brush into a pewter pitcher of turps and stomped over to the door in the well-worn half-boots I used for slippers. Probably another drunk. I shouted: Yes? I was about to grump back to my easel when he spoke.

Words bear the same relationship to truth that Roman numerals bear to Arab numbers—they get there badly. Maybe that's why you paint and I compose, he told the buzzer. Can you imagine saying that to a corroded buzzer? That's either faith or desperation.

I hadn't told him where I live. I leaned on the door with one hand, chomping my lower lip. Then I buzzed him in.

When he got to my landing three flights up he was walled up behind his eyes. He belonged somewhere else. I didn't motion him in.

Roman numerals trudge, Arabic numerals dance, he said.

I could see that for him this passed as urgency. I relented, nodded him in and headed for the stove to brew some drunk's bane. I don't know why it didn't occur to me that he was drunk. He wasn't.

But I'm not sure it's truth I'm after, he said. No, it feels to me I'm after what works. If I were to say I'm after truth I'd feel full of shit, wouldn't you? I'll settle for what works.

He was holding his tea saucer as if he expected it to float in air while he sipped. I felt it was a geometric feat that his bones fell into any kind of order. He looked like a study in chaos.

I was hooked. Artists are always after what works. I'd never liked and disliked anybody before. I doubted he was as presumptuous with anybody else, and I wondered what in me prompted it.

He kept his back to it as if he didn't want me to get between him and the door. He was trying to break free of the luggage of his words. He raised his voice so I'd hear him.

Yeah, he said, truth's kind of an alcoholic word. Grandiose. Music is about what works, but once in a while you hear something and you snatch it out of the air, like grasping a mosquito. It escapes from another dimension and you're in the right place to greet it. I owe everything to staying in the moment when no one else dares to be there. All the liars in the world are about fearing to be there. That's what politicians and critics are about—not being there. The moment is radiological, you can turn to Nagasaki dust in it—everybody knows this, which is why the present is the least inhabited place. It's the most dangerous. I drink to avoid it. But once in a while I have the guts to stand in it. Then I salute myself with a drink and the next day I survey the ruins.

I don't blame you. What can you do in it besides turning to dust?

Strike the right note, choose the right word, the right brush, glance, color, touch.

What's the right word?

Ascend. Stand in the moment and ascend.

Like him, like Christ?

A little.

That's what music's about? I don't know from music. A college friend told me I'd grow up when I preferred Mozart to Tchaikovsky.

Have you?

Grown up? It's my ambition. So far I'm going through the motions.

Music is about now. Not yesterday, not tomorrow. That's its power. It stops the spatial clock's tiresome plod from one point to another. Our sense of time is a convenience, a contraption. Music shows us that everything happens now. The past and the future are distractions. We welcome them because we're not up to the present.

Has it occurred to you that the mosquito you snatch out of the air you also kill?

His ass disappeared in my sofa, leaving only his knees to support his face.

That's the whole problem. What if we drink so we won't murder, or we murder only ourselves? Artists are killers. They see the moment nobody else sees and they kill it. All you're seeing, all you're hearing is this act of assassination. But you don't see the mosquito, you see a crushed bug. That's what art is, yours and mine. It's enough to make anyone drink.

I laughed so hard I started to pee.

Jesus, that's good. But you think I'm gonna swallow it? I was a drunk by the time I was fifteen, what the hell did I know about mosquitos or art or murder? What I knew was my mother thought I was a piece of shit and had ruined her life, that's what I knew. Every time she looked at me I saw the question in her face, Who are you? I've spent my whole life trying to answer her. But it's a rhetorical question. She knows who I am. I'm the person who ruined her life. And don't tell me you knew what you just said when you became a drunk. No, no, no. It just sounds too good. I love it. But it's full of shit, and you know it.

I poured foul coffee into the sink. I stared into the air shaft where I'd risked my neck installing a triptych of mirrors to funnel the sky into my galley and I found a face behind me that had no judgment in it. The Heron and I could go to bed or leave it, we could see each other or not, we could drink or not, because we were comrades in arms. It was comfortable to stand there watching him in the mirror watching me. There was no single thing we wanted from each other except this habit we'd fallen into of saying damned things. This habit we'd picked off each other like mushroom hunters in a wet forest.

When I turned he was inspecting the paintings on my walls, too polite to pull others from racks. I was born with this dangerous eye, and my face just focuses around it—I wanted to tell him that. He stopped at an apothecary trolley loaded with vodka and whiskey and cordials. He took out a handkerchief and began dusting my demons. His strange stewardship of my booze made me sweat.

I told him about my dangerous eye: I drink on the one hand to apologize for the eye and on the other hand to bear the pain of seeing how it roils people's bowels.

Yeah, that and a hundred other reasons, right?

I nodded.

Look, if you didn't have a dangerous eye only the galleries would want your paintings.

Did he mean what I thought he meant?

They want what they can sell, right? That means shit.

Is composing like that?

Life's like that. The Parisians threw bananas at Stravinsky.

But he saw fame in his lifetime, didn't he?

Yes, poor bastard. Me too. Doesn't mean a thing. I know perfectly well that music better than mine is being written and

22

not being heard. And I'm not sure I want to face up to that because it would make me too sad to write at all. Live with your dangerous eye, for better or worse. I don't have your courage, I live with a lie. The most important thing in life is not to blink.

Could I see it, his lie? I snatched a big sketchbook and led him over to a stool by a window, convinced I could catch his lie. It's what I do. It's why people bear down on me.

You're going to try to draw it out of me?

No, that's not the way it happens. People don't give up their lies and when they're caught with them on their faces they hate you for seeing them. The second face they see isn't the one you see. The one they see tells them the truth, the one you see is lying. They're caught as if they got tired holding up a mask on a stick at a masquerade. And the reason they hate you for seeing the face behind the face is that they know what they've sacrificed to get by in the world and they hate themselves for it. But we don't know what they've sacrificed. We're intruders. We've caught them in their bedrooms. We're as sorry as they are angry. There's no use telling them we've caught them with a remnant of the powers we give up to placate the satraps of this world. It sucks and we know it. It accounts for our conflicts with parents. They're the first ones who coax and bully our powers from us so we'll idolize pigs.

The rebel vein snaked down his forehead toward his left eye. He ground his teeth. Is it how he looks when he's about to walk out on a noodling lecturer? Or is it a rapist's look?

***

I hang my paintings on fish-line slings that slide along tracks in the ceiling. I hang them according to size. The result is that there are blocks of darkness between groups of paintings. The Heron got up as I spoke and started weaving in and out of these shadows. Sitting under a cluster of incandescents in the middle of my loft I felt stalked. The place became his, not mine. I wondered if his musicians felt the same way. Then I realized he was the victim and I think he heard my mind.

Would you mind if I pace around the outskirts of your studio?

23

he asked. I'll come back to the campfire and tell you a shameful story, but I have to collect it in the shadows. D'you mind?

It's a matter of principle with me not to answer manipulative questions. No matter what he did he couldn't shake an answer out of me.

I'm a Barbary pirate, he said when he returned to the campfire to pose for me, you can't get by me without paying tribute. I was scooting charcoal crumbs off my pad with my pinky and he didn't think he had my attention. He did need tribute. That's why I painted his face on his back. It was a Bronx cheer, and he knew it.

I particularly like to search women for their gems—he raised the ante. Their rubies, fire opals and pearls ....

A current of recognition started up my spine. How could he know the way I thought of my body, my personal gemology? How could he know the cross on which I hung? How could he know I thought myself crucified by my sexual attributes and dreamed of androgyny?

What do I call what's going on here? I asked myself. Rape? Art can be rape. Paintings can pillage or they can pilfer. I called in all my adventures from around the loft to answer this question. What do I call this thing? An epiphany. Call it an epiphany, my paintings shouted from the recesses of the loft. Sing hallelujah. No, I said, when I collected myself. It's rape. I'll call it rape and I'll pretend to be outraged. I'll call it a vulgar effort to eroticize the air between us and I'll fix him with a cobalt stare. That's what I'll do. He has no right to cherry-pick my mind.

My flat-line lips disappeared in contempt as I stared at him.

I'm sorry, he said, I was sneaking up to a confession. I really am a pirate. It's one thing to listen to folk music and elaborate, as Stravinsky and Dvorak did, but when you take someone's music, knowing they don't know how to set it down on paper or to play it on an instrument, then what have you done?

It was hard to get past my cooked-up indignation, hard to respond to this one thing he had to tell me.

I said, You can imitate an artist, you can forge a painting, but you can't lift an impulse that way, at least I don't think you can. So you feel you're a crook?

A very successful one. It's like the perfect heist. I live off my ill-gotten gains. I'll tell you about it.

I'm going to sketch you—is that okay?

What if I hate you for what you sketch?

Well, drunks trying to stay sober are supposed to face up to themselves, so if you see yourself, good luck. If you hate me, shame on you.

Sketch. I'll talk.

He could see I was again willing to listen. Sketch, he said, but he no sooner said it than he got off his stool and walked to the windows.

Can you hear me from here? Don't turn around, please. You mustn't see too much. There must be a distance, a caesura between us. To draw somebody confessing is to ask them to give up too much.

I was struggling to understand him. We listened to the traffic down on Broadway for a while. Then he said, Decency is like the statue of a goddess, she can't come home with you, she can't count on you. Can anybody?

You must leave what you see where you see it, he seemed to be saying. Not something an artist wants to hear, and yet every good artist knows it's true. He could only bear to tell me what he had to say from the shadows. I know a lot about Greek and Roman sculpture. I studied it a long time before I got up the nerve to sketch live models. Do you think the Greeks painted their statues so we could be hot for them? I asked him. Are we all pure and bland underneath, while our indecencies are painted on us? We're hot for illusions, aren't we? I'm never hot for my subjects, I'm hot for what I paint.

Can you mix pheromones into your paint?

If I could I'd never have to worry about shit-pot critics.

No, but you'd have a lot more to worry about. I don't think the Greeks knew about pheromones.

I think they did, in a certain way. You can't smell an Egyptian or Roman statue, but the Greeks were intimate with their gods. Their gods were often pricks and bitches. It's because their statues have been scoured by time they reek of ideas. But I suspect Diana once upon a time stank of piss and sweat and the unctions of her desires, and I suspect the hyacinth of Athena's reserve woke men hard in the morning, and the sea tang of Hermes twisted girls in their sleep, and....

Whoa! Let me see the paintings you've salted away behind the others.

Which are those?

The ones your fragrant gods told you to hide.

Hide? Everything I hide is in plain sight. That's how I became a drunk, to ease the pain of doing things in the open. How did you become a drunk?

To ease the pain of having nothing at all to say and wanting desperately to say something. I had this gift to understand sound but no gift to make it. I understood everything about music except how to write it. It's the heartbreak of Salieri, knowing you're always going to be second best.

You're just going to keep shoveling intellectual horse plop at me, aren't you? I don't believe for a minute that's why you're a drunk. I think you're glib. I know I'm glib. I could've been a poet, but not a good one. Nothing's as deadly to a drunk as glibness. Nobody's more ready to believe his own crap than a drunk. My newspaper friend tells me most of our laws are passed by falling-down drunks. I believe it, that's why we need lawyers to decipher them. They think if they haven't been drinking they're not drunk. And we don't know any better ourselves, do we? You're shitting me, wasting my time. You're shitting yourself, wasting your own time.

I wanted to love all the busy people, too busy for me. No, that sounds like Tchaikovsky. I wanted some fond summons to pass between us, a casual salute, the opposite of hard looks and stares. Vivaldi or Telemann working something out.

I got up and walked over to him. I put my hand on his

heart. Yes, I know the sense, I said. Renoir or maybe Seurat. Serene, familiar. No demons to feed. I don't want a life any more dramatic than a Rubens tit.

Flowing?

No, but willing. I've had a Giotto kind of life, flirting with grotesques. Look at the red in Giotto and you know what madness is. It's like blood in your eye.

You should aim higher. Seraphim for starters. Star beasts of species yet to be discovered.

I like you better when you talk about loving all the busy people, too busy for you. I like your fond summons and casual salute, I ...

I've always been called to the sorrow of women, but cold to my own, he said. I think God's a Jewish woman gagging on the breath of Cossacks. Her sound, the noise you remember her for, is klezmer, that heartbreaking plaint of the alienated. And don't go looking for it in the Oxford, you won't find it, because nobody's going to embrace it whose heart hasn't already been broken. So here I have my foreign broken-hearted God. What's happened to her omnipotence, you say? Do you say it? Well, you should. She's put it aside to indulge herself. Is she afraid of the Cossacks? She made them, didn't she? But we should be afraid of what we make, that's the point. We should sing heart-breaking songs about it. We should do a lot of things we don't, and this is the purpose of my foreign God. Do you think the Cossacks worry about her? No, they gave her the gift of blue eyes and fair children and think she should be grateful they didn't kill her. Do I know what I'm talking about? Absolutely not. I guarantee it. God is always a foreigner.

***

We were having a drunken conversation. But shards of sobriety stuck in our hides. I had a big problem with his eyes. Usually when I have a problem with the eyes I give mine a rest. Eyes are always a problem. They belie words and don't stay put. So I started sketching frantically, but then I noticed his eyes guttered and receded to something back in his head. I'd missed that about him. The Heron rarely blinked. He rarely searched the walls and ceiling while talking to me. He was listening. His words were incidental to other sounds. I loved it and began trying to catch it with charcoal and chalk. Whatever he said of his own dishonesty, he could be trusted. His eyes said so. He had listening eyes but they had trouble dealing with what they heard. You didn't always see them when you looked at him. They needed to rest. The light in them was a decoy fire to mislead you while he rested. He was calling himself a deceiver. As I worked on his face I remembered something I'd read about the wreckers of Hatteras. In storms they'd wave their lanterns at ships to lead them onto shoals, and when the ships foundered the wreckers looted them. The Heron was a wrecker. His eyes lured you onto the shoals. Then he looted you.

Watch it, be careful. This man calls words mean bastards making nice, and here he is, deploying them again like pawns on a chess board. I worked on his mouth. If I could get it right I'd be inured to the words coming out of it. The eyes were another matter. They had cavernous sockets. I'd have to get the sockets right first, then wait for the wrecker's light.

If you want to know the truth, he said—hah—you're going to tell me you want to know the truth, right?—nobody does. You do? And I should believe you?

I shadowed his side sinister—sinister because he was dissembling—with the flat of a charcoal and frisked him for more. I turned down the left side of his mouth and pulled it into shadows.

Okay, the truth in my life is a sideways elevator.

This is going to be rich, I thought.

No matter what button I punch, it goes sideways, usually right, sometimes left. When it goes left I get dizzy. I walk for days falling towards ten o'clock. The buttons are winking indecipherably in sequence. But they're hieroglyphs. I can't remember them. That's the truth. Well, it's a recurrent dream, and dreams are one way or another true. The only thing I know about this dream is that I have it when things go well. I suppose you could call it a *memento mori*. And when things go blah-duh-

28

dee-blah-blah-blah I dream I'm in a big sailboat making way in a stony stream bed. Yeah, you like that? Are the sails set? What a question! Actually it's a pretty good question. Why didn't I think of that? I don't know, it's not in the dream. I bet you they're flopping around in a light air on a hot day. You're not a sailor, are you? That's not ideal sailing weather.

I know a reporter for the *Times* who told me the way to interview people is to keep your mouth shut until they get desperate to fill the void and spill their guts. That works? I asked him, because I knew it wouldn't work on me. Well, yeah, he said, most of the time. But he told me he once interviewed Richard Helms, the spook, who found the silence restful. I think he told me that story because I reminded him of Helms. But unlike Helms I don't have beans to spill. I just don't like talking, which of course you're not going to believe if you hear this.

I don't have The Heron's sound memory, but I remember words, sometimes it seems like every damned one of them. And scenes, I remember scenes. Looks, especially looks. I must have given The Heron an odd one because he launched a riff:

There are no hummers or whistlers in *The Oxford Dictionary of Music*. No scat, no rap, no raï. Isadora Duncan's efforts to dance to symphonic music are ignored. So I feel confident that I've covered my tracks. My dirty little secret is safe in the snobbery of the establishment. I'm what the establishment wants a composer to be. It helps to look like what you aspire to be. It reaffirms the pooh-bahs' prejudices.

It helps him to look like a Giacometti bird? I thought.

I look like I ought to be famous, he said. I wear fame well. People are comfortable with it. It doesn't jab them in the eye. All my life people have clamored to crown me with the laurels I seem to deserve. As a young man I was desperate to deserve them. It's like the army, if you look like a general they fall all over themselves to make you one. If you lose a battle they blame it on paper pushers or politicians. Somehow I instinctively understood this. It amused me so much I wore it well, too well.

This was not bad as confessions go, but cagey. It was the

least I hoped for, something better than an AA meeting. But I couldn't snare him in a sidelong glance and that bothered me. I didn't like spending so much face time with a hidden face. Men and women who are truly fey can't be liked or disliked. They don't belong to the human race, so you can't rely on experience to peg them. I can't paint them. I don't think anyone can. Any attempt I've ever seen is Disneyesque. The Heron wasn't one of them, but he smelled of them, and that meant he did business with them. You can't get away with messing with them. So I let him talk about hummers and whistlers and throat singers, about sinus cavities, the head as an instrument, and auditory memory.

He kept discovering as he talked that he didn't want me. I kept being grateful. He was handsome in a silver way, hair and sinews freshets in the sun. But I've done handsome, I've done beautiful, I prefer strange.

I sketched him conducting our little suite. It upset me. I'm a musical illiterate, so I substituted numbers for musical notations.

That makes you a mathematician, I said, showing him my sketch. He rubbed his hands the way I do when I'm trying to decide which colors to mix.

Boogie-woogie's in the Oxford, he offered.

I started sketching his hands. They were beautiful. I wouldn't trust them with my body parts.

He saw that I sketched with distaste. He grimaced and took a big breath as if he were about to dive from a height.

When I was a kid in Manhattan, he began, I wore my rubber heels down in a month. You can walk off almost anything: suicide, blues, beatings, bullies, hateful adults and twenty kinds of rejection striking unforgettable notes in forgettable places. You can. I did.

He took off a pointy shoe. Look, he said, good as new. Now I drink instead of walking, or at least I did drink. Then he sighed again and walked over to my easel. He straightened a painting and came back and sat.

I look like I ought to be famous, he said. He did look like that.

I plumbed my molars with my tongue, wondering if my

sketch had caught his torment. You know, you do look as if you ought to be famous, I said, and it's nice the world obliges. But it's not quite that simple, is it? The way you look doesn't disquiet people. That's important nowadays.

Nowadays?

Yeah, we have a low tolerance for anybody whose looks don't dope us up. I once saw a mosaic fragment from Pompeii. It was Alexander the Great's face. He obsessed the Romans. There were those moon-shot eyes I'd seen in other representations of him. I think he probably looked scary as hell. Handsome, sure, but scary. And you can't do that unless you're born a prince and really do everything better than everyone else. You need a captive audience to be so unsettling. So what you didn't say is that you're not like that. Your looks aren't like aspirin on an empty stomach. I gave him one of those have-you-got-it looks.

I think the only thing he got was I was beginning to say something important to me. We say the right things to the wrong people. The people who need to hear us scare us. I scare enough people already. I was glad not to scare him. He was grateful I was telling him something, anything. I got bolder.

I was born behind my mother's back, I told him. My father divorced me instead of her. I don't feel welcome here. People always look like they can't place me. They can't. But they have the queasy feeling I can always place them.

My whole life I'd been trying to describe my mother's attitude towards me, and now finally I had. She always looked like I'd been born behind her back. My face reddened with this recognition. I skimmed my middle finger through the pond between my boobs and put it in my mouth. This was hard-won sweat. I remembered the ecstasy of my berserker forebears. Like them, the Vikings, I'd turned over the world order and it tasted good. Then I made a mistake. I handed over my power to him. I thought to myself, this guy is tripping my circuit-breakers. There's too much of him. I'm on overload. He had listened till I croaked something awful out of myself and now I was blaming him for it instead of celebrating.

31

Fire smoldered in the walls. That's what happens when you stop drinking. You smell the smoke and you have to poke smooth things. You know there's something acrid behind everything, everyone. Some people confront you with too much and you have to get rid of them. The only question then is the decency of how. I paint in the space between you and the invented you. It's the space where nobody wants you to be, so of course it's quite familiar. There are people who will do everything necessary to clean you out of that space. The Heron wasn't one of them. He reminded me that only occasionally do I paint the full figure. He reminded me because his own full figure lent itself to caricature, as if some wraith had flown through his midriff, leaving his head teetering on his knees.

Uh, look, some people....

Yes, I understand, he said. I do. We can only deal with so much. That leaves some of us out. Please take care of yourself.

Then he tied a shoe, snatched up his leather jacket and walked out. Black rain drove the dregs of winter down storm drains. I watched him lean into it as he crossed Broadway to the east. I knew he would quit my class. I felt relieved and defeated at the same time. Sending him away was an alcoholic thing to do, cheap and selfish. I'd seen him as a music-maker, but he was a listener. I was lost in my own empty quarter.

***

We navigate tides and currents of sendings. Something about being born behind your mother's back destroys your filters. You're always waiting for her to realize you're hers. The waiting ravishes you. Every sending smacks you like a wet mackerel. Everybody's feeling you up. You're where you don't want to be, knowing more than you need to know, much more.

You can't read the instruction manuals, you can't decode what comes your way. Everybody else can read them. Fuck it, fuck them all if they can't take a joke. Then you drink. You celebrate your desperation. For about an hour every day you feel like a Valkyrie. Then you feel worse than dead till three p.m. tomorrow, but at least you forget you can't read the manuals.

This is the sort of thing I could have been telling The Heron. But he'd become the listener I didn't want to be. I didn't want to hear that wretched little naked girl waiting for it to dawn on her mother who she was. I never want to hear her. What could she say at her age that would make sense?

I have a stained snapshot of me taken at age four in our back yard on a summer day. I'm looking anxiously at my mother, who is on a chaise longue. There can be no doubt in anybody's mind that if there were a talk balloon over my mother's head it would say, What're you looking at? Emphasis on you. Somebody has said it at least once to all of us, so we know how it feels. It feels like my relationship with my mother. When I showed up at Pratt the buildings smelled like some familiar trespass and every face said, What're you doing here? One day in my second year I slipped on some steps in the rain, but somehow I got to the bottom without breaking my neck and I turned around and shouted, But I can draw, you stupid pricks! Something kind of triumphant just got shaken out of me, and somehow I made it through school without cracking up, or maybe I was too drunk to notice I had cracked up. That can happen, you know. But I was right, I could draw, and most of them couldn't, them being pricks, men and women. Something a drunk can do for herself is recognize she's angry and enjoy the high, if it doesn't get her killed. I think that's what happened that rainy day. I enjoyed the high and realized it didn't necessarily have to get me killed. Also it helped being tall. You can get away with a lot of shit when you're tall. The Heron and I both knew that.

***

The Heron quit. The students in the second row of my class moved up to the first and I started going to AA meetings again. I was maladjusting pretty well when it dawned on me that he had poked into my work but I'd never heard a single note by him.

His work wasn't hard to find. Start with the *Zohar Suite*, a clerk at Tower suggested. In the picture on the back of the CD The Heron was conducting, looking as he had in our conversations, moving the words around with his hands, shaping them into thoughts around our heads. I thought he looked as if he was writing Arabic in the air. I liked this photograph. And I noticed he was trying to shin himself up off the ground. The Heron was ambitious to fly. I liked that too. So why isn't this on sale? I asked the clerk. He liked the question. Maybe because it isn't, he shrugged with a smile.

***

The Zohar is the pearl of Qaballah. The hairs on my body rose to transmit and receive as I listened to this suite named for it. I can't sing a note. I croak and wheeze. I can't play an instrument. But I like music in a stupid way. The *Zohar Suite* stunned me: every note was an electron navigating my blood on a secret mission. It was like the Qaballah. I'd been painting for hours when I remembered I never paint to music. The creator of this music couldn't bear touch or much of anything else. If I don't like the way a paint feels I don't use it. I once told a friend her paint didn't like her palette. It was a porcelain tray and the paint shrank back from it. It's the same with canvas and stretchers. I have a lot of contempt for artists who bully their materials. They're often the ones who get a lot of press. The press is about triumph, not celebration. It's about marshaling, marching—don't get me started.

There I was conducting the electrons, letting *The Zohar* paint, celebrating its mysteries. It was like realizing your perfect lover is a vampire. You pay for perfection. What did The Heron pay?

***

We were at our memorial tables in the Spice Cafe when I looked up into his face. He pointed to his heart, then to mine, and I nodded yes. He came over and sat.

I've been listening to your *Zohar Suite*. Actually I've been painting with it.

He smiled as if he understood and then he started as if he hadn't walked out one rainy night intending not to return.

Music is my sex, he said. When I was nineteen I began remembering how as an old man I pined for an erection. Blessed with such a baleful memory I turned to my music for sex. But

34

it wasn't mine. Mine rebukes, like the beauty of some women. It doesn't want to be intruded upon. I like it better in my head than on paper. But hers is changeable as weather. She has a huge larynx, a vagus that could have conducted *Das Rheingold*. And perfect pitch. D'you know how rare perfect pitch is? Her voice could burn out the diaphragm of a microphone. But I never heard her utter a word. I never asked if anyone had. I didn't want to know. I knew all I needed to know.

Who was he talking about? We hadn't been talking about any woman with a strange voice. How am I going to play this? I wondered.

Do you and the pining old man talk?

It's not necessary. I feel his disapproval.

Of?

The old man broke his pick on the hardest rock he could find. That's me living there up ahead. Pining. I'd do anything not to pine. For anyone. So I had to steal.

What? What did you steal?

Music. Not fame. Fools give you fame. I stole music. I stole her music.

I didn't want to hear this *her*. Whoever she was, she was my sister. I had no business consorting with somebody who'd robbed her. He'd begun to tell me his secret and I couldn't, wouldn't hear it. That's the way it is with us drunks. We're always waiting for something to happen, and when it does we hate it. Why is it we don't want to hear that one thing? I think it's because we want to choose the moment our life changes, so we end up like a batter struck out looking in the World Series. I looked at my watch and said I had to go. I didn't. We both knew that. But drunks are about control, and I had to get it back.

***

They always get the vampire wrong in movies. It doesn't matter who plays him, they get him wrong. He doesn't have that mesmerizing movie gaze; that's how he gets you. That's why he's so lovely to be around. He not only doesn't show up in the mirror, he is the mirror. All you see is yourself. You're not ready for him. You never are. I feel every gaze that taps me on the shoulder or undresses me in public, but I never felt The Heron's, so I felt lonely walking away from him, from the classes he no longer attended. He hadn't come to all of them, but he'd come often enough, even when I thought he wouldn't, and I could see he'd been sketching on his own, trying new crayons and pastels and chalks. I wanted to feel his gaze, yet I wanted to escape. He was like booze. He belonged in a drawing class. He needed tutoring. For all our compulsion to be rid of each other, we counted on each other being there. But where was that?

***

The dumber the country the lonelier its thoughtful remnant. I never wanted to be part of an elite, but my mother always stood at the door acting like I didn't have a ticket. She was the gate I couldn't get past, the family I didn't belong to. That sort of forces you into the thoughtful remnant. There's something wrong with you, you don't act like other people, she'd say. It seemed plausible. So the bigger she got, the smaller and lonelier I got. It didn't dawn on me until I started drawing that you can fill up a room with your own theatricality, which is what she did. I think I was drawn to art as a way of figuring out all the things and all the people I'm not like. I'm always trying to get in, so naturally I've never wanted to let anybody in. Some artists move paint around all their lives, but the paint never really lets them in. I used to think it was the nature of beauty to keep us out. I think if I'd ever been able to say that it might have gotten a smile out of my mother. It took me a long time to paint my way out of this notion. I've always thought myself lucky not to be homely. Beauty would have been too much responsibility. My mother didn't carry it off very well. She had an entourage, which of course meant most people weren't in it.

The first thing I didn't get as a child was my face. It was helpfully recognizable, but not special. So what did my mother mean about me not being like everybody else? What was everybody else like? I guess the special pain of wearing this face comes from its having been exiled by its creator. If she didn't like it, who was I to like it? I asked my maternal grandma about it one day and she took it between her palms and announced, It'll do. So there you had it. Grandma said It'll do, and there wasn't much she didn't know, including, as she told me the last week of her life, the awfulness of my mother. I took my grandmother's austere opinion of my face seriously. My face makes eyelids tic and lips twitch. I'm hard to look in the eye, and when men do turn on to me I always wonder if they want me to whip them. The women usually want me to protect them.

***

In The Heron's absence I began to think a man who was amused about wearing his face on his back might be worth knowing better. And then there was that remark about staying sober. We were both trying to stay sober. It wasn't easy. It never is. Actually sober's the wrong word. You can be off the sauce for decades and not be sober. Sober is something else. Once you stop boozing you have to start growing up, starting when you started drinking. So there I was two years ago, sitting in a circle in a meerschaum-colored parish hall, a fifteen-year-old trying to act adult. The severity of my face and my six-foot body helped me get away with it.

***

The Heron suggested our regular meetings one night at Cooper Union. I was walking behind him in a dim hall when he turned around and waited for me. You like drawing? I asked.

Yes, drawing. I'm afraid of color, but I like drawing.

It's the booze, don't you think?

Say what?

We drink to keep something in the bottle, something corked in our own bottled-up selves. Our craziness, our daring, our anger. Whatever. You keep color in the tube. You're afraid to let it out. That's alcoholic, right?

He sighed. Then he fell back and waited for me to turn around. You know, he said, we could keep each other company like Scheherazade and Shah Zeman. It'd be better than AA meetings, wouldn't it?

Sometimes when you're painting something you see the spirit living in it. Just for a moment, so your hand has to be quick. Not a sprite, but the intelligence that informs a thing. For example, you go out one morning intending to draw cornerstones. It's just an exercise, the kind I give students. Maybe I picked cornerstones because they're essential, unlike, say, cornices, which ice the cake. You notice their colors are different, their shapes. But after a while you feel the weight they're carrying, their sense of their own purpose, maybe even something about the day they were set in place. If you're good, if you're an artist. Otherwise, you just bring back a pad filled with cornerstones. So as we stood frozen in that dim corridor I saw that what The Heron and I had in common was an impulse to cut out formalities, to refrain from giving each other the runaround.

I mean, I say some sirloin face is a drunk and you say he has rosacea. That's a runaround. The Heron and I knew we were fellow drunks, always would be. You stop drinking, maybe, but you're still a drunk. Sure, there are telltale signs, but mostly you have to be willing to dispense with the bullshit. You have to be willing to jump across the grand canyon between you and everybody else, and when you get there you say, Here I am, and the other guy either says, There you are, or he says, You're in my face. So what we had in common was we understood that. He got it the night I painted his long, morbid face on his Albini shirt. And I got it when he just nodded as if it had been inevitable, like it's what an alcoholic teacher of a certain age at Cooper Union does.

So what's wrong with AA?

Nothing, he said, it's just… well, all those live sockets in moldy parish halls, and the occasional face I really don't want to spill my guts to. I get lonely there. Lonelier than I am when I'm home alone. Does that make sense?

If I didn't like a man who'd say such a thing, well, then I ought to like him. I often feel like a live socket myself. None of us like to admit how lonely we are. None of us likes to admit there are times when everything you touch shocks you.

So who'll be Scheherazade and who the easily bored schmuck?

You be the schmuck, he said. I'll start.

Hah, not interested in the gender issue. I liked that. Couldn't care less about it myself. We agreed to meet in my loft Tuesday evenings at eight. We shook hands, two storks in the reedy gloaming. I proposed we sketch as we talked. I sometimes teach private students in my loft. They and models are my usual guests, my society.

Artists come to New York City to meet each other, to meet gallery owners and curators and critics, to promote themselves, to network, as they say these days. This means lots of parties. Parties punish me. I can't process them, they come back like reflux. Each face comes at me like The Number Five Express. It's not going to stop at my station. And once I stopped drinking, parties started looking like toxic waste dumps. I went to a lot of movies when I first stopped drinking. Sometimes I had to rush out because I didn't have the filters to protect me from the onslaught. It taught me that I'd never had enough filters to deal with ordinary society. Everything is too intense, like a movie. I have enough trouble with the day's rushes. Outtakes elude me. I can't edit my life. I have to keep it stark. I have to keep the projector from overheating. I go crazy just looking at pictures of jungles. I prefer the old black and white movies. I can see more. The color doesn't bug up my eye. Have you ever noticed the way they used to handle scene transitions by having someone go over to a tray of bottles and pour a stiff one? If you're going to have to deal with a new scene you're definitely going to need a drink, right?

My deal with The Heron chilled my bones the moment I made it. It felt like one of those bad ideas whose inherent dread you just can't resist, like marrying the wrong person just to harelip the world. Our first meeting was on a wet spring night in late April, but I almost froze to death walking from Astor Place to lower Broadway in SoHo. I was still shivering in the pure wrongness of it when he arrived that first Tuesday. He had a big new sketchbook under arm and he seemed to have lost his head in a blue raincoat. I had the notion he might not emerge from it. Then I had the better notion it wasn't my problem. That's always a good notion for an alcoholic to have—let God fix the other guy's problems.

No sooner had our little deal started than he broke it. He buzzed my loft the next night as if I expected him. He wanted to say what he'd begun to say. Usually what people tell you they could tell anyone, even when it's announced with a fanfare. But once in a while you're the only one. And once in a great while they ask your permission first. Usually they strip-search you with a hard confidence. It was about her, the one with the larynx, he wanted to talk about her, and I already felt so heartbroken for her that I'd begun to hate him without reason.

You can tell me who she is. I'm giving you permission.

He stood at the gate of hell, in this case my doorway. I'd opened the door and walked away into the fires of his hell. It was the perfect moment in a B movie from the fifties for me to pour that drink. I could hear the camera whirring. I like movies where the director listens for the sound of his actors' minds. Of course he has to choose his actors carefully. The Heron's mind sounded like an orchestra before the curtain rises: shuffling, scraping, coughing, tuning.

I wasn't sure he'd heard me, he seemed so deafened by his own misery. You can tell me who she is, I said again. I wasn't sure he could do it. We listened to the city. We listened to our blood. We both knew this moment wouldn't come again.

I wish I knew, he said. I don't know who she is. I know what she looks like. I know how she sounds. But I don't know who she is, and at the same time I know better than anybody else. I can't ....

I flew at him to put my hand over his mouth, and when I felt his body sob under touch I made a priestly little cross with my forefinger on his forehead. Then I found a large sketchbook, bigger than the one he'd been using, and told him, Draw her and I'll draw you, which is hard to do, hologram that you are.

He smiled, a stitchy little scratch across his rocky face. He liked the idea of being a hologram, I could tell.

He drew a square-faced lioness. You can read a lot of color into black and white. It's subtler than a color photograph. If you looked at this face too long you couldn't get back to your own dimension. Would that be fine with you? I found her hard to look at. I'd never before seen anyone who so much wanted nothing. I blew a whoosh of wonderment.

Yeah, he said.

He'd drawn her kneeling. You wouldn't give a pope or a king her gaze unless you were mad. They always want something, and you want something from them, which is their power, so you paint them as they wish to be, you fawn, and down the centuries comes that lie. But there was something else in this lioness's face—she was ready for anything.

Is this the look Christ gave Pilate, do you think? The look that got him killed? The look that still comes thundering down the ages.

Well, he said, if it had been in Woodstock it would've gotten him a roach.

I looked at him as if he smelled bad. My look stung him. If you lay something that heavy on someone and they deal with it, you owe them more than a cheap quip.

He explored each of my loft's three factory windows. They blaze and cry and buzz with Manhattan's toils. He touched them like a prisoner looking for loose mortar. Then he turned towards me and started talking as he approached.

There's a place—it's somewhere in Manhattan nobody will ever find—that I visit in my dreams. It's a big rectangle the size of Gramercy Park, but its axis is north-south and it's paved with Florentine geometries of bricks—arcs and squares within squares, every earthen fancy you can imagine. It is framed by churches. Brunelleschis, Christopher Wrens, all of them. Gothic and Romanesque and Byzantine. This place, this piazza is usually

41

empty, silent as nuclear winter. It's where I come from, where I'm going. Last night I went there and it was filled with long, watery El Greco beings. I think they're seen only when they consent to be seen. The bells were ringing. I think the people were leaving the churches. They weren't talking or gesticulating. I had the notion they didn't need to, ever. I was standing on one side of the piazza, the east side—you can imagine this place in the Fifties between Fifth and Sixth—and I started shinning myself on thin air. It was funny, because I do that, sort of, when I'm conducting and I want to imbue the orchestra with the idea that we're about to go somewhere else and I want them to lay down what we've just played. I shinned until I felt my feet leave the beautiful brickwork, and in seconds I was hovering around the rose window of one of the Wrens, and then I was up by its tower and I saw myself waving a long red scarf like an angel in a Shipley. I was there in my skin but I was also observing myself from the east side of the piazza. I kept getting smaller and more distant and then I woke up and cried. I was furious to wake up. I was mad for the dream, for the piazza, for my place in the sky, waving a scarf.

What were you wearing?

That's just the right question, you know. Everyone wore pendant scarves and garlands of flowers. They didn't walk, they flowed. And I think they were sexless, or they could be any sex. That would be lovely, wouldn't it? Wouldn't....

He was going to go on but he saw the sweat gleam on my upper lip and the blastedness of my look. I went to a row of old paintings, the ones I didn't think deserved fishline cradles. I pulled out an old canvas from my student days, forty by thirty inches. It was grimy. I half expected silverfish to dart out from under its stretchers. But it was The Heron's piazza. Down to the brickwork, but depopulated, as post-apocalyptic as a de Chirico. In the instant before I turned to hold it up to him I knew how God feels—desolate. We look for better company, we insist we owe him nothing and go about our business.

He stared at my painting, his piazza, for a few seconds. You, he said matter-of-factly. You, he said again, and left. Again.

***

This is the pattern of most marriages. None of us can bear too much of each other. So why not come and go? But what did I know of marriage? I can't stand anybody long enough to live with them and the feeling has always been mutual. I like people in their place, in paintings. I don't know how or if they like me, and it's been a blessing not to care too much, unlike The Heron. Drinking blurs his caring. A drunk's concern is a lie. That's why I figured he'd come back, if not Tuesday, then Wednesday, and if not Wednesday someday, because he'd gone to great length to tell me and not to tell me about her. And the piazza in the midtown of his mind and my happening to have it stowed away in my student stuff was just a sly cowardly diversion, like our alcoholism.

***

I think he'd been trying to figure out when I frequented the cafe. Maybe he even asked the people who worked there. Maybe they even told him. He sat down without being invited. First of all, he said, I don't think I can stand you for a thousand and one nights. I can't stand anybody that long. Can you? Okay, so we agreed about that. Maybe we could both play Scheherazade. That way I get to play with my anima, you get to play with your animus and we keep the schmuck happy. Otherwise he's going to lop off our heads. It could work. We're too grand, the two of us, to go to AA and sit around kegeling with a lot of dank strangers. So we swap stories in the faint hope it will keep us out of the bottle. That's it, see? The schmuck's the booze. The difference between us and Scheherazade is we don't want to end up with him, even if he is the shah of Persia. You don't want to end up with me, I don't want to end up with you, and we're going to have to kill Shah Zeman. Otherwise we'll end up pausing in the middle of a story and pouring a drink, so the cameraman can figure out what to do next. We agree to go deep, right? The alternative is to bore ourselves back into the bottle. Problem number one: I don't want to go deep. Do you? Okay, that's why we have to, because we don't want to. Problem

43

number two: I do want to go deep but not with you. Problem number three, assuming we can overcome problem number two, is who goes first? We could flip a coin. Heads you first, tails me first. Which brings me back to problem number two: why not you? Could I beat around the bush? Whose bush? Sexy retort. How 'bout yours? Okay, here I go head first. But I have to teeter on the springboard for a while. I have to calm down, get on top of my language—it's too flip, you know, bar-room jive, you think you're saying something profound and you're full of it. I have to calm down. I want to talk thoughtfully. I'd like to talk thoughtfully. It's frightening. Do you agree? Good, this is good—we're in agreement about—I have to shut up, shut up and think.

He sounded like a schizophrenic babbling on a table while the nurse prepares a hypodermic to calm him down. Schizophrenics hear people think. They say they do, anyway, and I believe them. The Heron was talking as if he knew what I was thinking, as if he'd known all along. I was mulling over the possibility of feeling frightened about this when I recognized that it's exactly how I treated him. Aha, two nuts had unerringly found each other.

I like that, I said. The part about you shutting up. You're drunk. That's the problem. This shit about who goes first, we've already settled that. You're drunk, got it? So you haven't been drinking, so what? You're drunk. You're not behaving soberly. I'm a solitary drunk. You're not. You're a barroom crock. That's what you're doing now. I don't like it. Go away. When you want to sit and sketch, we'll talk. But I don't think you have anything to say until you tell me about her. I don't want to hear about her, but that's what you have to say, and it's all you have to say.

But that's not the deal, he said.

It's my deal. I get to change things. I get not to answer questions I don't like.

He made an arabesque with his hand in the air, a signature flourish, the arrest of an orchestra. He meant it as a stop, but it came off like a dismissal.

Very well. I nodded. Then I borrowed a page from him.

When you sketch or paint someone, I said, they usually project themselves. They prefer you to feel like a camera. You don't want to feel like a camera. You don't want to sketch their sense of self. At least I don't. It doesn't interest me. Their lives are devoted to it. I want to catch the self they've suborned. I think that's the right word. Yes, what they're showing me is a misdeed. I want to see the person they accompanied to this awful place, the one who consented to arrive in a blurt of blood to be put in the hands of... the suborners. But then there are the few people whom my reassuring hands and intent lull back into some original state, their state when tragically they consented to come here. I live to see them, no one else. They're the only people I want to paint.

As I searched him for signs of recognition I saw the loneliness of Pan, fucker of goats and seducer of the nascent. But Pan wasn't equal to the task. He kept on playing his pipes, unwilling to tell his secret, to speak of her, because if he did, then what? What would stand between him and the booze? Confession is good for the soul only when it doesn't kill you. Or maybe it's better if it does. Being in doubt moved him to blather. Blather he did:

The beauty of some women is a gut punch and a klaxon, he rehearsed. They sport their purest outside faces and win the hearts of all who don't care. I say leave them to sculptors. Just keep looking at me. Hold me still. I'm trying to say it right. Okay, then there are women whose flaws were put in all the right places by a devil. That's it. Thank you. Hold me still. A devil. They suck the blood up out of your shoes. I want to do things to these women. Don't turn away. Hold me. You're not like them. No, you're like the women who have to be left to sculptors. I don't want to do anything to you. Listen, I've never said this to anyone—how could I?—these women, the ones with the viral flaws, I know the demon who made them. I kept him drunk in my basement, clawing the walls and rattling the bars. He's out now and I want to tell these women what I want to do to them. Dirty things. Don't let me stop. You've no idea how important this is. I never had the nerve, drunk or sober. I'm a limp dick in a suit. Did you hear that? You have nothing to fear from me. Bullshit? You think it's bullshit? I get it, you have to fear, or it won't mean anything. Yes, it's about power, yes, it's about control. If you'd been raped and nearly hung when you were a child, you'd... I'm sorry, I don't know what you'd do, do I? No, I don't. If you could just keep looking at me, you know, looking but not staring, and if you could keep your face blank I could finish this, I could confess. Thank you. Look, we could do it this way: heads you tell me something dirty you'd like to do to me or somebody else, and tails I tell you. Why does it have to be dirty? There's a question Baudelaire would've liked. I think it has to be dirty—for me, maybe not you—because the dirtiness of my thoughts is what is armored the most. If the dirt were exposed, I'd be exposed as the alien posing as one of you. Or not. That's why flipping a coin is so apt. You're wondering if I'm going to get to the catch in the proposition, aren't you? You're right, nobody wins. If you agree to play the game, I won't want to play it with you. If you don't agree, I'll do something filthy to you in my head. The premise of games is suspect: in the act of winning we lose the enticement. I want to pick the petals off Baudelaire's flowers of evil. Have you noticed they don't sound so sinister in English? The relationship of musical notation to language is intriguing. One would think notation is a lingua franca, but do you think the Brandenburg Concerti would sound the same if Bach had thought in English?

I knew what he meant by dirty thoughts, things pornographers stop short of, but the problem is nothing ever strikes me as dirty. I don't get the word unless it's limited to grime, something I can wipe up or grind into paint. I'm too tactile. But I know what others mean by it. I don't know what it is we shouldn't do unless it's to harm one another. I don't understand debates about what harms and what doesn't. They're liars' debates, aren't they? I mean, we know what harms. We know. But we pretend not to know in order to fit in, to be accepted. The trouble is we don't fit in, any of us. But most of us are determined to try, so we end up killing Jews and anybody else we can cut out from the pack.

Killing them makes us think we belong. He wants me to agree to tell him dirty things. What if I think they're lovely things? He'll be crushed, won't he? It won't help to keep him sober. And what will help to keep me sober? Certainly not telling him the ways I masturbate.

I know what you're talking about, I told him. It bores me, this business of dirty things. What's dirty? What idea, what fantasy, what? I like everything you say except the dirty secrets you say you want to expose. It's like dirty underwear, I suppose, more interesting because it's dirty. Look, I understand the use of this word, I do, but I don't like it. It's not a hot button for me, it's a fart. We have lots of thoughts, don't we, that we don't share because we can't know if the other person will like them. You say you're a limp dick in a suit and that's supposed to reassure me. I say I have a face you'd have to be odd to be hot for. Is that supposed to reassure you? We don't have each other's hot buttons in us. That's what makes it possible for us to keep each other company, to help each other stay sober, maybe even to help each other take a few steps towards adulthood. But I don't think you can talk to an artist about what's dirty. Not really. If I can't paint it or paint with it, I'm not interested in it. When the Nazis or the Soviets called a certain kind of art decadent, it was just words acting up. Nothing's decadent except the boobs telling us what is. If you want to deposit a dirty thought with me, I'm sure it won't trouble me any more than my childhood yen to be my best friend's panties.

That was the end of that. He smiled gratefully and said, You never show the class any of your paintings.

***

We sat as if we'd been killed and couldn't believe it. Our silences were precarious. We didn't inspire generosity in each other. What we wanted from each other could only come from ourselves. Maybe that's always true, everywhere, with everyone.

I paint these big blocks of flat color, I said finally.

Hofmann? he said.

Yeah, I studied with him. Then I work between the cracks.

47

What goes on there is secret. We say things to dramatize them—so-and-so or such-and-such drove me to drink—but I think it's easier to drink than face the sheer damn meanness of what goes on between the cracks. I think that's a certain kind of truth we'd do almost anything not to face. When I come out from between the cracks I'm shell-shocked. Now they call it post-traumatic stress. Nobody stops by my bed to pin a medal on me. My paintings are my campaign ribbons. The first time I heard someone say in a movie, I need a drink, it sounded like an answered prayer. That's what I need, I told myself, I need a drink, I deserve a drink. You know what I said to myself when I heard about Dr. Josef Mengele at Auschwitz? I said I know all about him. I knew all about people sticking their fingers in me for my own good. I knew all about my own good. I knew all about people talking about my own good as if they gave a damn. And that's the one thing I wanted to paint—the difference between what they say and what they do. And don't think you can't paint it. You look hard enough at anyone and you'll see the difference, and if you don't, well, there's a person whose fingers you don't have to worry about, a person I spend extra time painting because I feel love. And I'm not just talking about figurative painting. It could be squiggles, dots, blobs, geometrics, it ....

There's a lot that peeves you?

I shook the tears out of my eyes.

Yes, I said, young women pushing strollers like battering rams/ people hanging up without saying goodbye/people walking in a phalanx on a crowded street and refusing to make way/fish-eyed cashiers who field complaints with, I only work here, or, That's not my job, or, You'll have to call so-and-so—and what you have to call is an endless telephone tree that tells you nobody gives a shit what you have to say or what you'll ever have to say.... Does anybody think such a society is good for anybody except crooks with briefcases? Yeah, and having an arthritic pinky is very bad for wiping your ass. But there's a lot I like. I saw a woman of a certain age in fake leopard. She was skiing on slush on Fifth Avenue followed by her Lhasa Apso in his little fake leopard coat and boots.

The Heron was a baby handed a shiny bauble. His words were usually marquee bulbs blinking. It was hard to find his slate eyes. But now they came out of their caves.

I always play QXR for my books, my recordings, so they won't be lonely. I don't like anything glib, he said. Youth is glib, don't you think? Smooth. You have to fish for character because nothing really stands out. Character in youth is erotic. The rest is just what one projects on a pretty face. I like travertine marble, it's poignant, it's laid down by forgotten springs. I'm sick to death of asking women what's wrong. As if I didn't know. They've foolishly wasted their time on me, that's what's wrong. And even if they suspect I know it, they don't begin to suspect that I know it's their function in life to waste their time on men. Don't get me wrong, I don't mean all women. No, just the ones I myself have foolishly wasted my time on. I like that look on your face. Bemusement. If I asked you what's wrong, you'd tell me. The ones who don't tell you are complicit.

Everyone looks at big splotches of things. Everyone pays attention to people who want attention. Why is that? We miss everything when we do that. The big splotches are just taking up space. Big splotches, celebrity, fame, it's not where the action is. The action's in the cracks. I was working him into the cracks, and I found him obedient material.

He nodded as if he got it. We smiled in concert. You can get along mechanically with someone yet not be in concert. Two people find themselves in the same slipstream only rarely. I took up his sketchpad from where it leaned on his chair and set it in his lap. Then I handed him a couple of pencils from my pocket. He looked up as if he were going to sketch me and said,

Conceit bears the virus of malaise. I'm quoting myself at Gould Hall. I think I said, Listen to Salieri, he's always trumping himself. You hear the lack of confidence behind his conceit. A young man in the front row stared at me intently, shaking his head. You don't get it, do you? I asked. He was too intent on getting it to be embarrassed. Are you studying music? I asked him. Violin, he said. You have the essential quality of a great musician, I told him—humility. Listen to Bach. Hear that certitude? It doesn't come from your own praises. No, no, it's God's answer to your own prayer, to your music. His face lit up. I climbed off the stage and shook his hand, and he had the courage to hold my hand for a moment. When I think of Bach I think of mathematicians: you can't lure a true mathematician away from his certainties, not even with glory.

About those blocks of color, what're you doing in your abstract paintings, the ones that are not portraits?

I'm working in the cracks. The big blocs of color are events staged to punctuate what goes on. It's the way we write history, the way we keep time, marching from splotch to splotch in a circle. But if you go down into the cracks, knowing that you might not come back, you may find some of the beauty with which you arrived here, some of the innocence.

They're like tectonic valleys. Composers understand tectonics.

I don't. I think they're spaces that open between dimensions. I don't think everyone sees them. It depends on how much you remember. I think maybe drinking is like trying to glue them shut when they start opening out. I think booze is our defense against powers we don't know how to cope with. But I find every day terrifying, so I look for the cracks as if they were exit signs in a theater fire. In the cracks I use my palette knife, pencil points, styluses, string, mineral dusts. I'm determined to convey that what's really going on is not what we think is going on, and it's not where we think it's going on. News is distraction, diversion. History's a slant of wars, governments, leaders and discoveries. Everyone and everything glorified is less than those lives that go unnoticed. The more facts television moons at us the more illiterate and stupefied we are. The more we see the less we observe. So if one of my paintings can arrest the eye for a moment, it can point the mind into the cracks. What's going on never makes the news. The news is what blinds us to what's going on.

I saw his several minds thrash in his face. I grabbed a sketchpad from the chair next to me and began penciling them. The ideas engaged him, but they were inconvenient. He had only one thing to say. It was doubtful he'd say it. He thought it fortunate there aren't too many like me in the world. But meeting me seemed less than accidental, so it troubled him. He lifted an invisible orchestra to its feet with his hands and then began speaking animatedly,

If you really want to appreciate a play you have to go two or three times to watch how the actors inhabit the words. Every night the body and the word get to know each other better and they change each other. Directors should hire artists to sketch rehearsals, to massage the body into the word.

He looked at me eagerly when he'd finished. I wanted to shake him the way you clasp a lover's shoulders and cry incredulously, You!—as if you can't believe such a one exists, not only exists but exists for you. Better yet, he knew I wanted to do it. But it would have pushed us into a realm we'd not agreed to, and because it might not be a sober realm it was too much to risk. Or maybe we wouldn't be able to go there without a little drinkypoo. So I poured my thumb into my empty cup to signal the waitress and told him a story.

***

We were studying the Qaballah, I began. Our teacher, David, asked us the week before to think about sharing one of the fruits of our meditations. I'd scribbled something in the subway the day before. Our teacher wrung his hands in anticipation. I'd brought a little wooden box and I fetched it from my coat and brought it back to the middle of the floor where we sat in a circle. I'd transferred my little subway donnée to rice paper in gold ink, rolled it like an ancient papyrus and put it in the box. I thought it deserved a little elegance because it plopped into my head whole. I carry a copy around with me because the thought tries to escape me. I'll read it to you. Tell me if you feel it trying to get away from you.

***

Nature holds bones and ashes with respect, but our artifacts usually end up in the wrong hands. We smile from photographs into the wrong faces from the wrong bureaus. Our handwriting marches against someone's wont. Our books, so fondly gathered, are sold for a pittance. Those with whom we shared the most sacred moments are disinherited from our remains. Not only lovers and would-be lovers, but passing strangers in whom once we glimpsed the truth of our own being. They should have had these things from us, but instead we endure among the grievances of those we thought we ought to love and those who thought they ought to love us. To be in the right place at the right time with the right person is at least half the oneness mystics crave, but don't tell them.

Don't tell them, David mused. It delighted him. No, of course not, don't tell them, he cried, because it will only earn some pretentious platitude. Never tell them, because if you know them to be mystics, if they've led you to believe they are, they're not, count on it. He beamed at me the rest of the evening. The usual smiles rippled from face to face until my eyes found a newcomer in our assembly. Newcomers come and go. There were three that night. This man's gravitas caught David's eye and the two of them sat engrossed in some sort of recognition. Don't tell them, David told this man. Never, he said, looking at the stranger as if he were the only one in the room who understood, even though we all acted as if we did. David's eyes followed me fondly when I left.

It anticipates our death, The Heron said. What's left of us will be in the wrong hands, won't it?

Usually, I said.

Well, the music and the paintings, we can't do much about them, but they're not as important as the invisible, incorporeal gifts we leave. Did you ever speak to the stranger in David's class?

No, nor did David. But that gift, the one that passed between them, it does more work in the world than our music and paintings. He's the person most of us don't see. Or we see him for a moment and shake the moment out of our heads. He's that violin student who held your hand. He came out of the crack and went back into it.

It was working, we'd agreed on that, hadn't we? We were entertaining the schmuck and keeping our heads. Well, we were wrong. Any time you tear something out of your heart and put it in somebody's hands your life's at risk no matter how grand a thing it is to do. In any event it was out of the box, something torn from my heart. Not that I knew what it was. I just knew it should be preserved. For what? When I die somebody will clean up and throw it away. My life will end up in thirty-gallon black bags on the street.

Actually, that's sort of what The Heron did. He sat for a few moments, taking in the story about the stranger in the Qaballah class, then he rose, looked at me as if I were a complete stranger, put down some money and left, leaving his sketchpad on the table. I sat wondering what I felt and then knowing I felt the fitness of it. I should have told that story and he should have left. It's the way I feel about the paintings I still like a year or two after I paint them, the ones whose inevitability left me no room to celebrate when I finished them.

The great work of our endangered sobriety was finished just like that, because I had the temerity to share something dear, because he couldn't handle it, whatever it was, because we'd embarked on a venture so fragile it could drown in a snowflake. It happens, I'd seen it happen before. You're compelled to say something and whoosh, the person you say it to vanishes, like when I told my old friend Alice, You have a grand compulsion to be offended by me. Where did it come from, that jugular observation? It hardly felt like it came from me at all, but it did and I never saw Alice again. I might as well have slugged her head with a sledgehammer. I wonder if there are paintings like that hammer. I think there are—Francis Bacon, Lucien Freud—I'm sure there are. Right, it's not just the ones you want to see again and again that are good. It's also the ones that mug you. So I mugged The Heron. My friend The Heron? Can I say that? He didn't feel like a friend, but I valued him. So how 'bout a little hair of the dog to celebrate another dead-bang observation straight from the loneliness of Pan? Yup, that's right. I once saw a statue of Pan fucking a goat and I thought it sure is lonely when you do what you do. Well, that's not all I thought, I thought what a modest prick for a god. But it was a Roman statue and you can't expect a Roman sculptor to be as awed by a god as a Greek. Someone told me you lose all your friends when you sober up either because in the cold light of the street you don't like them or they don't like you, and in any case none of you are what you thought you were. Sobriety's a whole new ball game and whoever told you it was fun was drunk. It sucks, but I was getting hooked on the terror of it. You never know what's going to happen when you're sober, and if you can get to see that it's an adventure, then you're not such a shut-in any more, because that's what a drunk is, you know, a shut-in—stuck in his own bonko bin and persuading himself how much he likes it every time he takes another drink. Sure, there are solitary drunks and there are corner-tavern whiners and bullshitters. But they're shut-ins trying to control their tiny environments.

So I walked home slowly, ritually made myself a pot of green tea and said a little prayer for The Heron with an earless Japanese cup in my hands.

***

I've known stars of royal entrances and exits. My mother was one. She processed from scene to scene among her courtiers and subjects. She took up room she never earned. She stole too much air, leaving everybody gasping. In her presence I was wallpaper. But The Heron opened and closed spaces surgically. He followed the Hippocratic oath, do no harm. So I understood with more certainty than I have about life in general that he'd be back to tell me about her and then I wouldn't be needed any more. I had nothing so imperative to tell him. And in any event I didn't trust him enough to tell him any such thing. But he'd enriched my life. His angle of vision was as strange as my own. Our encounter would play out between the cracks where

I work. I can't say that of many people. They slide off me as most viewers slide off the surface of my colors. The cracks between them are interstices, not worlds. That's how they live, on the surface. If this were a book or a catalogue I could show you what I mean. As it is, I'll send you to see the paintings of Nicolas de Staël or Bradley Walker Tomlin. I'm indebted to people I don't trust. Petty tyrants like my mother taught me where the hooks are. They show me how I get hooked and driven crazy. No, wait a minute, I apologize, I'm lying. If what I say were true I wouldn't be a drunk. At most the tyrants have taught me how to sanitize the hooks in alcohol. They're not as infectious that way, but of course the alcohol kills you.

So Shah Zeman waited to hear about the woman with perfect pitch, waited in the wings. The Heron just went on performing, showing off, moving words and sounds around, orchestrating, postponing, interjecting a fermata here and there. What was he postponing? Telling me about her, of course. But what would it cost him?

**

Then I got, got, got... what did I get? An illuminated text in a lovely pickled-gray box mailed to Cooper Union as if he'd forgotten my address. It was like getting a dozen roses from a guy you dumped. You want him to stay dumped, to respect it. I couldn't wipe the irritation off my face. A rectangle had been carved into the cover of the box and tooled with gold leaf. Onto this the leitmotif of the *Zohar Suite* had been painted in green. I don't read music. I had to ask a friend to sing it wordlessly. I resented this gift-wrapping of what he had to say. The idea came from me and I felt ripped off. To hell with this silver bastard. I wasn't going to open the damned box dolling up what he didn't have the nerve to tell me. Walk it down to the river and send it out to the Fresh Kills, I thought. I liked that thought so much it dampened my anger. I could have found him. After all, he enrolled in my class, he taught at Juilliard. But it seems to me a person who doesn't want to be found is entitled, unless... he's committed a crime, he's entitled not to be found... it's becoming hard to vanish in our society, isn't it? Our data doesn't belong to us only. The Heron is an outlaw, I told myself. I understood this very well. It's bound up in his drunkenness. He thinks, like all alcoholics, he can get away with it. My mother was an outlaw. She thought her beauty and grace were a free pass, a license to ignore the rules by which most of us play. Fair play was for the booboisie. There's a subterranean vein of this outlaw mind in the right wing. Fuck the poor if they can't take a joke. Fuck you all, why should society be burdened by you? We're ruled by Bible-blathering pirates now. Their selfishness is worse for the ozone layer than fluorocarbons. Like the emperor Commodus, they stockpile weapons of mass distraction, counting on us not to notice rape and pillage wrapped in the flag.

What can I say? I amused myself with tirades against the electorate while I stared at The Heron's pickled gray box. Any time a drunk vents anger there's a possibility, however slim, she might just glimpse the hero's way. She might just look in the mirror with her toothbrush stuck in her mouth and say, Do you think it might be possible to grow up before you die? Do you think you might just like that? Yes, of course it will scare the shit out of you, but maybe that would be fun compared to the sheer damned pain of wearing the wrong face. But the chances are better that for a second she'll see nothing in the mirror and go scrambling in a bureau for a face, any face to get through the day, because in the sober distance is a loneliness too great for anyone to risk.

But you're risking it, I told the mirror. Day by day, you're risking it, inching up on the terrible loneliness, the truth that you've never been welcome here, never. So what, I shouted at the mirror one morning, spitting the brush out of my rabid mouth, so the hell what? Then I opened the box.

I think he probably wrote his music with the same broad nib. He'd found deckled brown paper and wrote in green ink. After certain sentences he wrote a few musical notes. But there was none in the margins or between the paragraphs. The first page was a feathery pencil sketch of a naked man conducting an orchestra. He drew with a clean wry line, like Thurber. I loved it. I wished he'd drawn everything so I wouldn't have to read.

***

The first time I saw her, he started, *she shook a tambourine at me from across Mill Hill Road. Woodstock's a town where people pop capillaries calling attention to themselves. Tattoos, mohawks, camouflage, scruffy beards, ponytails, grit, stink, hysterical talk, theatrical embraces are all enlisted in the cause. Pretensions to privacy smell of narcissism. But this woman was translucent. She didn't want to be seen but she most certainly saw. I knew a lot about her the moment I saw her. I think that's why she shook her tambourine at me, to warn me that she knew.*

You're in this place of bloated psyches, then suddenly there's this person who doesn't need any room. Every time I saw her I fell in her direction. It was like standing at the center of a big clock and seeing the cosmos between 10 and 11. The minutes are gone. So that's where you have to go, between 10 and 11. And if you do, there'll be nothing to return to, you won't be able to re-enter the circle, the belt around our lives. Time chases itself, but she was outside the chase. There has never been anybody waiting for me, needing me, so it seemed a good place to go, the only place to go, but where was it? I think that's why they followed Jesus, the disciples—everybody was taking up too much room and he didn't want any at all.

Back and forth The Heron went with his showy nib, between second and first person, you and I. I didn't care about him, I cared about her, and I shared this in common with him. So I read on.

I found myself biking down from my hutch in Shady to the village to glimpse her sitting on a bench on the green, emerging from a shop shaping a peak of ice cream with her tongue, picking a newspaper out of the trash, sitting on steps watching weekenders board a bus Sunday evening, standing in a crowd listening to drummers. Blue and white is all she wore. Blue coveralls and white T-shirt, or white pants and a blue denim shirt. The moment she felt herself watched she vanished. It wasn't always me, others watched her too. She was tall and seemed to finger-paint herself on the air. If I hadn't seen others watch her I wouldn't've bet she was real. I ransacked my memory for someone she resembled to rid myself of the notion that she was a wraith. The more I spied on her the more she disquieted me. She could not be followed. In a hodgepodge of slapdash buildings chopped up by a quarrel of streets she managed to disappear in all weathers, walls and traffic being no obstacle.

Only because I value the company of the dead I heard her. Only because we both enjoy their company. I was fond of the Artists' Cemetery. Uphill the dead are upright, reciting their names, the history of the place—the Palatines, the Dutch, the Yankees. Downhill the artists, writers and musicians lie flat so the mower can clear them. They are forever flatland foreigners. Not being upright, they're low-maintenance. At the top of the hill is a high stone memorial wall with benches under it overseeing the town. I liked to sit in their company envying what if anything they knew.

Some people say they've heard the music of the djinn in Algeria, in the south where the Tuaregs live. The most plausible explanation is that they hear music from Bedouin encampments, but few who hear it believe that. Or it could be the wind and sand scouring the gorges and mesas. Few believe that either, and they die longing to hear it again. I've never heard the djinn. But I heard her from over and around the stone slab, humming, nasalizing, keening, throat-singing, whistling, moaning. I shut my eyes and heard this ensemble, melodies and refrains never before heard, stillborn sonatas. No sound I'd ever heard, not a voice or an instrument, came from such a pure place. I named a cantata after the place and called it Otherwhere. Pure is the only word I can think to describe it. Not pure the way we describe Bach, meaning mathematical, free of connotation. I mean pure, absolute the way a child is before she looks into her mother's eyes and takes her chances. No instrument is quite like a human, but I didn't believe a human could make these sounds, marrying them and divorcing them like a child sifting sand. A composer would have to resort to art to achieve pale hints of her melodies. And just as she took up no space in the world she took no possession of her music. She didn't seem to remember her melodies from day to day. I went slinking away down the hill tasting salt in the corner of my mouth. I wanted fame, she wanted nothing and was by far the better musician. I had followed her to a bad pass within myself.

58

But when the world can't resist dumping its laurels on you it's hard to believe you don't deserve them. So the only thing I could think to do about this woman was to save the sounds she made. Wasn't it noble of me?—I can hear your derision. You're right. They didn't need any saving. I wanted them. Not for posterity, but for me. I wanted them to be mine. I'm not an archivist. But thieves and burglars and plagiarists have their signatures, their characteristic way of doing things. A simple tape recorder would have been best for this espionage—I thought of that right away—but the idea offended me. If I was going to steal this woman's work I ought to do it elegantly. The enterprise deserved a touch of class. And since she wanted nothing, why should I give her anything? What would she take? The symmetry was compelling. By the time I got to the bottom of that hill, by the time I stood at the feet of all my fellow artists, my tears were whetting my appetite for fraud. More than that, I felt righteous because I had the perspicuity to grasp the situation, to shoulder my duty to rescue her work from the implosion of her life. As I write I savor your contempt. You will recognize the wet-brain thinking, my own contempt for myself and those who lavish praise on me. Contempt is so terrible a thing because nobody deserves it, not even the worst of us. It's our excuse for not being willing to grapple with the meannesses that have crippled us. Okay, you're right, I'm bullshitting again.

***

I balked. I took a walk around the loft. He was saying anything not to say what counts. Like your average politician. He gets to the bone when he draws. I envied him. He runs away, but he keeps his part of our bargain. How to keep mine? He's very good at sandbagging people, isn't he? I never met anyone I liked to dislike as much. But I can't feel contempt for a fellow drunk trying to salvage what's left, trying to grow up. Not many of us make it, if you define making it as staying alive five or ten more years. But growing up?—none of us quite makes it. We start too late too far behind, we don't live long enough, we're too handicapped. Somebody please tell me I'm wrong. He confesses to me. Who am I confessing to? Who is she singing to?—that's the question, isn't it? This illumination he sent me, it's that it isn't about us, it's about her.

59

He told me that for the last ten years he'd been building what he called a toothpick fantasy one hundred miles upriver in Woodstock. The town has a new-age sheen, he told me, that's one of the most famous cover-ups in the world. The place is a huge musical instrument whose major chord is anger. The rock musicians all know this. They play against it. It's the real energy of the town. It's what the hippies call the vibe. Of course they think it's a good vibe. And maybe it is.

So, fool, what are you doing up there wasting your time and money? I picked up his scroll hoping I was about to find out. A stave full of signs and symbols started his next paragraph. I'd have to get my friend to sound his notation again. He knew that. He wraps passive aggression as a gift, strewing my emerald-green way to the wraith with roadblocks.

The cemetery was surrounded on three sides with woods and brooks. I hid my bike in a stream bed in back of Vasco Pini, frame maker. That way I could enter the woods on the north side and avoid the dirt road up to the cemetery. I did this for a couple of days, poking around. Then one day I found blue and white clothing neatly folded in the crotch of an elm. I found small cairns made of the stone rubble the Yankee farmers buried in trenches when they dismantled their walls. She lived in these woods, bathed in these brooks, on the edge of a clamorous village. She lived with the dead in the carnival of those who come to be seen. I couldn't sneak up on her radar. I would have to choreograph something. I decided I would accustom her to my visits to the della Robbia dedicated to Ralph Whitehead, the xenophobe who founded the Byrdcliff arts and crafts colony, the eyebrow of the village. She would think I came to pay homage. I even set an occasional rose down on the stones in front of his della Robbia, contemplating that all these exotic names would have made his shorts itch. But from that distance it was hard to tell when she'd taken up position behind the monument at the top of the hill. The wind didn't often carry her fledgling sonatas from the southeast. But on still days or a kind wind I would hear her and I would steal up the hill over memorial sentiments to sit on the other side of the monument and jot down her wordless songs. She had her dimension and I had mine. She was on the side of the upright and I was on the side of the mown. No matter how much I wanted to keep on making notes I always stole down that hill while she was still singing so that, if she looked, she would see me sitting by the della Robbia. But I don't know if she ever looked. I don't know if she would have cared if she had known what I was doing. I don't know anything about her, but I know more than anybody.

And back at my shanty I started to score her work. Its habitudes and logic and strangeness consumed me. If I could do it, if I could keep on eavesdropping and noting and scoring, I'd have something the world would play and be changed by. Day by day she pulled me over to her dimension, just as the Zohar calls you out of dogma into the grandeur of mysticism. It was sacred what I was doing, like the ritual rape of a priestess. I glowed with the inevitability of the project. I was fragrant with its justness. I always thought happiness was a martinet saying, Are you happy now? Now I knew it was sitting on the other side of that fifteen-foot wall receiving ambrosia from that priestess. It came on the air, moist and scented with the profane. The ancient chief rabbis went into the holy of holies once a year with a rope tied around them so they would be able to come back. This woman came back and forth at will. She knew the holy of holies better than she knew this dreadful place to which we've been exiled. She didn't need any rope around her.

He ended his report with a musical notation that struck me as a barred window. It didn't occur to him that he was tying the rope, that he, the sacred thief, was the rope. Worlds don't occur to a drunk. It's the purpose of being drunk, so such things won't scare you. I think we're governed by drunks. I know them when I see them. Maybe they don't drink, but they're not sober. They put on religion to put us on, to make an end run around the awful job of growing up. A hundred years from now when people wonder about this time in our country I hope they'll see it wasn't a sober time. All this self-righteous greed sounds drunk as hell to me.

***

So it was out of the box. Like hell. He'd tarted up his story so much you'd think it was about him. The seam of the ordinary ripped, I heard it. Then for two months I heard nothing of him.

It felt right but it bothered me. There are certain people by whom we account for ourselves. They seduce the uncertain child in us and assume an importance to which they're not entitled. They've interfered with her, people used to say. He'd interfered with me, he'd interfered with her. We can't do without these interferers. But I felt he deserved the concern I wasn't willing to give him because he entrusted his shame to me, his misery. And besides, how many people tell a good story? Mostly they spritz you with trivia. The Internet helps them hide. They drown their souls in minutiae and invite you to applaud their sociability. They chuck things at you—apocrypha, bad art, dumb jokes, off-color stories—and call it communicating.

***

A box is for keeping things in, isn't it? said David, my qaballist. What does your friend want to keep in the box? You know, I said, I think it's me. I know that's crazy, but I think it's me. I think he wants me to know about her but not to care. I feel conned.

Sure, but don't you think he's sharp enough to guess that's how you'd feel? You're not going to draw it for me, are you? No, that wouldn't be any fun. You've been conned, but I wonder for how long.

Turns out The Heron mugged me too. He hit me with something about SoHo, my hometown, because that's the way Manhattan is, only pieces of it are your hometown. SoHo's mine. The invisible piazza is his. He said SoHo is a bad place to show art because it's remorseless. It festoons its sinister past—murderous fires and sweat shops—with banners and flags and haute couture. It daubs a painted face on the dark history behind its iron fronts. He said the elevator shafts in the backs of the lofts go straight to hell. Very bad for artists, those cables slapping in the night.

I told him he was a goddam snob to imply that artists are pollyanna mystifiers.

He looked shocked. But he liked a good idea too much to be dismissive. Yes, I guess even Francisco Goya has been unable to rescue me from my snobbery.

I liked that myself.

***

The box soon started crowding me out of my loft. I couldn't think of anything but the cables slapping in the night. I don't know much about music. I like jazz because I sense it's about coping. But I knew that what's good about his music is that it knows how you need to be upset. Heroes are allegories for the kind of courage I hear in his music. Cheap celebrity allegories. Real heroes die obscure.

I didn't miss The Heron, but I thought he ought to be in the world somewhere and I needed to know where. I thought I had a right to know where, and I didn't want to leave her to him. She wasn't safe. This man was one of those criminals destined to get away with their crimes. You can see their luck on them. It photographs well. When they're seventy they look forty-five. We're born to them, we marry them, we lust for them, we crown them, but we never get anything from them, except sorrow.

***

Not blinking at a hard thing makes an illusion of loss. I had a teacher ten years ago who used to talk to the class as if she were talking to me. And I knew why. It wasn't sexual. It was my gaze. I've seen it in wolves waiting for scraps in the Alberta pre-dawn. She liked it. And one day, looking straight at me, she said, The eye corrupts everything, none of us sees the same thing. And we're corrupted by what we see, I blurted out. Yes, like children, she said. Don't blink, whatever you do, don't blink, she said. Be like Goya, like Giotto. They blindfold the condemned for their executioners' sakes.

I can move away from those elevator cables. But I can't get away from what my teacher said. I know that not blinking makes an illusion of loss. I get that much. And now I think I see that it's not loss, it's our own truth slipping in and spooking us. And that's when you start growing up or not. Drinking is only one of the distractions at hand to fill the space your truth is attacking. We can shop and lie, hate and slander, climb over each other to get to the exit, be celebrated and die famous, but what do we celebrate?— not often the simple courage to grow up and die well.

I know this because I remember how strangely I felt when I read that only humans, apes, elephants and dolphins recognize their images in a mirror. Where does that leave me? I wondered. I have to get reacquainted with myself every morning. I can't brush my teeth without looking in a mirror; I have to be sure whose teeth are getting brushed.

***

Most cultured Victorians knew how to draw. I don't care if artists can draw. But that's only because I don't insist on knowing what art is. I do think art on paper is neglected. When the Frick put up a show of Parmigianino's drawings I got on a first-name basis with the guards. Drawing isn't a preliminary. It captures the moments that change everything. It's not just a matter of knowing your craft. Drawing goes to some bone-glimpse you've lived your life for. A good draughtsman doesn't blink at a hard thing. Consider Daumier. I never told The Heron—too stingy—I draw better than I paint. and he draws better than I do. Paint is mixed up with booze for me. I daub, glob, smear, plaster, plop, scrape, scoop, pour, spread, stroke—anything to make up for what I lose when I go from a sketch to a painting. But what really happens in the interlude between the drawn and painted is that I scuttle an illusion and have to scamper about for a hope, a plan to fill up the emptiness. Then there's the plain fact that only the rarest collector pays the big bucks for a drawing. The art market is like the diamond market. There's no intrinsic value in diamonds. They're not as precious as emeralds, but De Beers invented a diamond economy. Art is like that. Go to the right parties, stay sober enough to charm the right people, win over a critic or two, and the next thing you know you're hot. Maybe you deserve it, maybe not. But it doesn't matter. You're hot if the right people say you are. But no color, no fame. Paint's like booze, glossing over, covering up, containing, medicating the truth. And each of our truths is more awful than the next. Blinking and scampering, we hold God at bay. Or we entertain the illusion we can. It's like leaving your gifts at a birthday party. You don't want to owe anybody. It's an adolescent thing. I'd like not blinking to be my estate. Some inheritances are too terrible to bear—that's what my teacher meant about the eye corrupting what it sees—precognition, clairvoyance—drinking, we renounce them, we shut them down to shuffle through the world poorer than we were born. My inheritance is my wolfish eye. It takes a lot of booze to dim it. To grow up I have to think about paint all over again. I'll have to teach more, spend my grandmother's money less, and draw the world out. Sometimes I think we become drunks to do our parents' bidding. They taught us we're not gods, and we drink to remind ourselves they're right. You got it exactly backwards! Someone shouted at me at an AA meeting when I tried out that idea. We drink to feel like gods, he said. Yeah, for an hour or two, I said. I think both ideas are true.

***

The Heron calls words mean bastards making nice. I think colors are stark raving mad. The one thing an artist doesn't want to do is cure them. The mind of paint out of the tube is innocent. You can molest it or you can conspire with it in sacred places. I never mix paint on a killing surface, like a porcelain tray or a cheap plaque of wood. I can make white lucent in my palm. I can work sea froth into green on my thigh. I can make blue dizzy on my forearm. I can make orange burn and smoke on my belly. But not every day. Not if my own essences and moods dissemble. Not if the paints are too cold, too warm or distracted by invisible disorders.

I wait for materials to invite me to the dance. That's why I need a big space. They're dervishes. They let me consort with them. Sometimes they dance without me. I just sit in their midst and dream of flying. Sometimes they draw me into the dance. They know that I know stretchers have a grain, canvas has a wont, paint has a will. I'm not the choreographer or the alchemist. I'm a witness. They know I try not to force an outcome. I try to stop a good thing before it becomes an overdone thing. My skin senses what colors want. The shadows of my body speak to the paint. I know what's going to pull across a canvas in a certain way by the way it crosses my belly. I don't tell anybody this. I don't want it to end up in a press kit. It's important not to betray the confidences of your materials. That's why we gasp at Parmigianino's drawings: they are themselves that single moment when recognition lit the artist's eye and his materials were caught up in it. You could say that of all good drawing, and no one could argue with you, but the alchemical wedding of an artist to his materials is rare. Usually what we're seeing is a prenuptial agreement.

* * *

I didn't really want to find The Heron. We'd set each other on roads worth taking. We did our best by each other, and it was hardly good enough. I didn't want to see him. But I listened to his music, music I would never have heard if he weren't a thief. I listened. Others listened. And he had his fame, climbing over others to the exit. I couldn't imagine his pain, but I could imagine that he hadn't caused her any pain. It didn't seem to me there was anything to do except find him.

* * *

Hey, I said to one of my students, a guitarist, can you let me hear these notes? We sat in Tompkins Square Park and he thrummed The Heron's notes. At first they seemed alien to him, then he started picking through them. He found the tonic chord, the fragmentary notes, the coda. He tried several times before falling in with the notations. Finally he slapped his guitar and asked me if I'd like him to record them. No, thank you, I said.

When somebody says *You* as if they hadn't really recognized you before, it comes to you that maybe you're not familiar with the person they've seen. Once The Heron said it to me I mimicked every possible way it could be said. You bitch, you marvel, you genius, you liar, you goddess. But the speaker was gone, Juilliard didn't know where. He'd taken a sabbatical, they said. His students didn't know where, the waiters at the Spice Cafe hadn't seen him. His phone was unlisted. Juilliard was protective. There was no listing for him in the 845 area code, which includes Woodstock.

***

The principal business of most Woodstockers is being seen. All that gorgeous self-concern can grind you into dog chow pretty fast. Eccentricity's one thing, I like it, but when you dial it up and strut it around, it cloys. For a painter interested in micro-expressions the town is a shit-out-of-luck place.

I parked my aging and pampered Norton Commando in front of a shop called Pondicherry on the village green. It immediately drew a group of tweakers. The Heron wasn't a rocker, so I didn't think it would do much good to ask them how to find him. He called himself a necropolitan, so I figured cemeteries were a good place to start.

I took a room on the third floor of The Colony Arts Center, an improbable Moorish whimsy, after observing that the town's two cemeteries were its most important neighbors. I took my time, sketching a cupola here, a capital there, trying not to call attention to myself—a fool's errand in a town of fragile egoists. I had the dead in mind, but they're used to waiting. I started a few pop 'n' lock moves on Rock City Road one evening to the rhythms of kids drumming with sticks inside a huge corrugated conduit that was going to carry off flood waters. My toes pointed me up cemetery hill. The Dutch and Palatines and English sitting with their backs to the setting sun struck me more as slacker sentinels than greeters. I greeted a few by name as guilelessly as I could. The artists, writers and musicians are the steppingstones descending the other side of the hill. Their headstones are obliged to lie flat, suggesting perhaps a greater degree of death than the settlers'. It's supposed to make it easy to mow grass, but you can't help thinking they weren't seen as important as the others, being outsiders, Jews, Reds, atheists, uninvited tourists. Barely tolerated, they'd made the town famous and now they're well hidden and mowed down for their trouble. But they'd had fun, some of them, done a lot of carousing, some of them, and even done some important things. There's Robert Starer, the composer. Anton Refregier, the artist, and quite a few other important people.

I decided to pretend I was a *plein air* artist and I set up in the cemetery. I wasn't interested in landscape. The Hudson River school with all its triumphalism feels like goose paté in my stomach. The art I saw around this famous art colony made my teeth hurt. Worse yet, it was St. Patrick's Day, not my favorite day, even though I'm half Irish. Few people in the world are as belligerently one thing as the Irish. When they celebrate St. Patrick's Day what they're really celebrating is how many of the rest of us are not Irish. I'm not wild about my German side for similar reasons. I always figured the safest place to spend St. Patrick's Day in New York is Little Italy.

***

The shadows of trees and hawks played on the untracked snow. She wore a faded blue Apache head-scarf and a white sailor's jumper with a blue eagle and two red chevrons over white painter's pants. Her lavender aura wavered in the half-light. She was the one. I knew it. She was what the town's flagrant notice-me's were not. I thought that if I pretended to be doing something long enough she'd come to feed on it like the leeriest bird. I was right because in two days she stepped out of a rhododendron copse toweling her honey-colored hair. She studied me from about eight feet, her green eyes haunting her eyelashes. She was in her late thirties, early forties, lithe as a whip. I thought it would be a bad idea to speak or even nod. I pointed to the pastel I was noodling about and turned up my hands and shrugged. She came over, examined it and then sat down cross-legged at the foot of my tripod. I tore the page off, crumpled it, and stuffed it in a pocket. Then I started to sketch her.

The dumb show was too pleasant to hurry. I waited a long while before I spoke. I'm going to use charcoal and chalk, I told her, because you haven't brought your color with you today.

I have to take care of it, you don't know what people are going to do, she said.

Yes, I understand, you're like a submarine rigging for silent running.

What do they do?

They have a procedure for running silently, no dishes rattling, no talking, no shuffling around, things like that. Like you, they don't want to be seen or heard except on their own terms. But they're not like you, because their job is to harm people and your job is not to be harmed.

It was too late to tell her that, much too late.

She came every day for seven days. Then it rained. I went to the cemetery anyway and sat under a white pine on a stone bench at the artists' feet. She came up behind me silent as dew, sat down next to me and handed me a green apple.

I brought it with me today, she said.

I studied her face and said, Yes, lavender.

I know who you're looking for, she said.

We sat listening to some Sufi drummers not far away.

He flew away, she said.

We listened to the drummers. They make a lot of noise, she said. I don't like it.

Her presence was like humidity, her aftereffect clement. I called her Boots. It made her smile. I glanced at her tatty boots. She asked me to buy her a pair of boots. She didn't ask me if I would, she asked me to buy them. I felt honored and bought her a good pair.

They live on the edge of madness, they can hardly stand it. That's why I sing. To get it out of me so I can stand it.

Not the Sufis, she didn't mean them, she meant the rest of us.

Are you a musician?

I sing, but I don't use words. Words are like penguins. They don't belong here. You don't bother me.

Do most people bother you?

They hurt. Slaps, and whips in the air. They're crows, they steal your shiny things and carry them away.

Listen, Boots, there's such a thing as a micro-expression. It flickers across the face so fast maybe one in a million people see it. Those people know what you think and what you feel and they know you'll do everything you can to make them

69

think they're wrong. They live on the edge of madness. They can hardly stand it. They're the children whose caretakers played now-you-see-it-now-you-don't.

Nothing in the austerity of her speech encouraged me to think she'd know what I was talking about. But her lavender aura wasn't bought on the cheap.

I sing so I can stand what I see, she said.

They all did something like that, I said, waving my hand over the dead artists. I gave her three pastel and chalk portraits of herself.

Where's yours?

I paint like you sing.

I don't think she knew how to smile any more. But after staring ahead for a minute or two she stood up and faced me and lifted up her jumper, exposing upturned breasts of such reticence that I caught my breath. Her straight thin lips were barely parted. Her eyes greened her Slav cheekbones. I passed my forefinger across her lips and then reached into my pocket for a handful of pastels. With them I made arabesques on her breasts. I made a green eye of her navel. I desired her. I wanted to paint her body every day into the near future.

***

You wear your choices. The one thing a face disguises is the past life that drives this one to its challenges. If you've risen to any of these challenges it shows on your face. If you haven't it shows as vapid beauty or a purple nose or tricky lips. No one's as stunningly arid as a narcissist, you're not going to get anything warm and wet out of one. I paint choices. I could see the one choice Boots wasn't going to make again, not in this life, was to be shut in a building, in a mind or a will. Hers was the lock-picker of songs, one long anthem to freedom.

You need boots too, she said one day. It had been three weeks since I bought her some. I knew she slept in trees and caressed the heavens with her fingertips. I knew her accent wouldn't incur patrician distaste. I knew her feet turned out in a Balanchine way. And I knew a juncture had been reached and passed and her face was set to finish it. The Heron and his coy box had brought me to her, to my sister.

***

He said he never heard her say a word. The more I thought about that the more I thought about his crime. The more I thought about his crime the more I thought about art as appropriation. I wondered if the abstractionists Moholy-Nagy and Albers and Hofmann somewhere in the back of their minds gave up on art as appropriation. I wondered if the obscenity of theft and control pulled them away from figurative painting, veered them towards abstraction. Whatever you wrest from a person you paint is a curse. But what you accept from their bounty is a gift. It's sacred. The viewer will know it. If you share loot with the viewer the critics will praise you, but you'll die badly. I don't like painting nudes, it's too easy to profane them. You ought to make a fair exchange with your subject. You're taking something of them away with you, what do they have of you? It has to be the fairness of your gaze. Otherwise you've both done badly. I'd never tell the tastemakers this, they'd hold it against me. But I've shared it with a few students. The tastemakers want to know what you've done differently from everyone else. And they want to know how many times you can do it again. It's the bogus standard of a materialistic world. It's like a best-seller list, the only thing it tells you is who is the bullshitter and the bullshitted. To know who's ahead is to know nothing.

***

I bought boots and started wearing them. I remembered that The Heron sat on the stone bench at the top of the hill listening to her. I visited the yew chapel where she must have sat singing. Maybe if I sat up there she'd say something about him. But this was not a woman who missed any of life's subtleties. She'd seen my boots and told me what she wanted to tell me. So I kept on painting her by the della Robbia. She'd lift up her shirt and I'd make a new eye of her navel. I gave her Kufic breasts and hieroglyphic buttocks. I made roses on her knees and Siberian irises on her arms. In the shadows of her groin swam the creatures of the deep and creatures no one had ever seen before. In time—mid-June by then—I realized I'd never been so happy. My sable brushes made her smile, sterner brushes made her tremble. And when our enterprise reached an exquisite crisis, when we felt the dead applaud, I invited her to paint me. She gave my navel a crown of thorns and whorled it into a vortex. From my pubis tears of milk and blood ran down my thighs. She took a long time choosing brushes and wet them in her mouth. I lifted my shirt and dropped my pants and turned in her hands as she wanted me, and not until I got back to my room did I look. I looked and was amazed. Thorns are not easy to paint, nor are tears of blood and milk. But the thorns looked bitter and the milk and blood ran luminously almost to my knees. In the mirror I saw sunbursts on my butt and water lilies on the backs of my legs. My calves were starry nights. I touched myself with love and yearning. How had she acquired such skill without the impulse to use it? But she had used it, on me. I bathed in an old claw-footed tub, she bathed in a rushing stream, and we met each day in the fervid laps of the dead to celebrate. But what? Ourselves?

What are we celebrating, d'you think? I asked her.

She came behind me, pressing, and cupped my stingy tits in her hands. See where they're pointing? Come.

They were pointing north. I decided to follow them. I packed my paint box, folded my easel and hid them in her yew chapel. I was afraid to take the time to bring them back to my room, afraid to break the spell. We set out, painted and booted sisters. She fetched water bottles from a hedgerow cache. D'you always follow them? I asked.

Boobs are pretty reliable if you don't send them any dumb messages. You missed the snake, you know. She ran a finger up the small of my back. I'll make another one.

We started walking up Rock City Road on bluestone slabs heaved up by the trees that guarded the town's other cemetery, the one whose citizens had been more welcome. I saw a bluebird flash where there were no knotholes for nests and took it as a good omen. Our arms brushed, we were brush familiars, but we kept a certain distance. It was a cool day, but I looked forward to the heat of our climb drawing out our body spices.

We'd never asked or given our names. I was happy about that because I don't like knowing the names of people who interest me. Their names are somebody else's business, a complication, a piece of bravado. Her privacy was lovely to me. The Greeks were wrong to paint their gods, wrong the way tattoos are wrong. Presumptuous. But painting a body and being privileged to do it again tomorrow is sacred. The goddess brings herself to you but she doesn't give herself, and nothing you do endures. If I were talking to The Heron I'd tell him this, but he's a thief and there's no need to say such things to a goddess.

Once we reached the Buddhist monastery on Mead's Mountain her body became more fluid. The guardedness of village living fell away. The road became a rocky trail, gullied, steep and winding. She leaped over the first washout and held out her hand. I was almost as agile as she but I wanted to hold her hand. It was strong and I felt she was launching me into the air. A great valley opened on one side of the trail and I had to fight the urge to careen out over it.

We left worn-out time below us. We swilled bottled water and peed exuberantly. I imagined I had silver blood, quick and unpredictable.

The tone holes of her vertebras reminded me of an oboe. I ran my fingers behind her groin to taste her sweat. She took no notice, it being natural anyone following her would want to do it.

We followed our tits. I had no idea why we were climbing this mountain that broods over Woodstock. I didn't even know its name. But I knew that what's interesting about a place is not what loose tongues want to tell you. She owned all I needed to know. Not a single stone was dislodged as she climbed. It was as if she did it every day and knew exactly where each footfall belonged. I was dying to taste the silver rills her sweat made in the sun. When we stopped at a ruined staircase she painted my mouth with sweat she drew from under her ghostly breasts. I thought of a bluebird bringing a grub home to a fledgling. I licked my lips and we went on.

***

They built a grand hotel here in the twenties. They ran out of money and the local people pillaged it during the war. They stole everything. Their houses are filled with things they took— mirrors, lintels, mantels, faucets, doorknobs, hundreds of things. But nobody talks about it. They say a fire destroyed it in 1946, but they know they ruined it long before the fire. That's how it is. We know things, but we tell a different story. Everything is a different story. That's why I don't use words. He knew that. That's a lot to know about a person,

She struck me dumb. She'd never strung two sentences together before. I had no reason to think she couldn't, I just believed she wouldn't. And I believed that any word that came out of me now would shut her down. I wet my finger in her navel and stuck it my mouth. This was our liturgy, the way we animated the gods. And she spoke again.

He thought he had to save the sounds. He thought he'd found his work, his purpose. I could hear the pages of his notebook turn. It made me cry. Then he'd sneak away so I wouldn't know what he was doing. If he'd thought about it he would've known better. But he was eager to get it down. You could be greedy for worse things, couldn't you? It wasn't a bad thing. I'm used to being heard. Bears and bobcats, possums and raccoons, deer and the other bums hear me. I know when they like it and when it hurts their ears. I can't do it in the open because I started doing it under my bed or in a closet. I'd cover my ears and hum. The first people I didn't want to hear were my mother and father. Their words were fancy and all their sentences parsed, but they were savages. After a while all the mean words I heard and all the ugly scenes I saw started playing in my head and I couldn't stop them. I couldn't air out my head. They were stuck in there. So I closed my eyes and I covered my ears and I hummed, but I could feel the walls closing in and the ceiling and the floor squeezing me. It started when I was very young, but I made it through Yale with all its suck-ups and the assholes who need them.

I got in her face. Our noses touched. I bathed in her sea-green air. I know who you are, Boots, I said. You're the limit of words. They're mean bastards making nice—that's what he said, Boots. You're the angel of limits, the limits of everything. He thought he was stealing fire from the gods in the place where we end and they begin.

We left the ruin behind us. After a while the trail forked. One fork led to a tarn called Echo Lake. We took the other one and came to a giant ledge overlooking the Hudson Valley. He told me what he did, she said. He asked me if I was angry. I touched his face like this, with the back of my hand. Then I pushed him. He smiled at me like a baby in his crib watching a whirligig. Then he turned and flew away like a heron, slowly.

We sat and watched a carousel of eagles ride the thermals. And then we got up and left the limit of everything. And went down hand in hand into the warm night of words and paints and sounds and pretense.

***

When I die burn me into ash, toss me into the air and photograph me as a tattered cloud, but I don't know yet what I'm going to do with this tape. The decent thing to do is to take it into the fire with me. Who'll want it? Who'll care? Who'll want the photograph? We want only money and fame. There's no one who ought to have this story when I'm gone, and if I'm wrong, who'll dispute me? We are each other's lost opportunities. Very few of us can say we spent our lives with the right people, but some of us can say we made the best of it anyway..

BOOK 2

GRACE

Art is a revolt against fate.

—André Malraux

Men blather about the perfidy of women. Sixteen-year-old Grace Torrance doesn't know about that, but she knows her exclamatory booblets, whoa-goddam legs and ultramarine eyes can get her in more trouble than she's already had from blatherers and daddy creeps. So the first thing she does with her pocket change is buy a pair of coveralls and a loose denim shirt at Modell's.

Sleeping arrangements come harder. The first nine nights in Manhattan she sleeps in rock shafts in the Freedom Tunnel leading from Penn Station to points north. Chris "Freedom" Pape and other graffiti artists had turned it into a museum. Bolts of natural light illuminate their work, and at night the homeless bivouac in this flip-the-bird museum.

Grace feels safer here than in Arendskill. That first night, as she huddles in the roots of utilities conduits, her mangy blue parka over her head, The Queen visits her crèche. Nobody calls her Queenie, nobody knows her name, and nobody ever hears a sound from her. She's almost a giant. Her eyes are holes of December sky. She hands Grace a flap of cold pizza, crouches in front of her and stares. Grace touches the Queen's tow hair. Her subjects rustle behind the queen. They've never seen anyone touch her.

A train rattles their bones, each mustard window taking someone somewhere. She can move on. She doesn't have to go back to her unsafe bed. The troutful Arendskill had gone on a rampage, tearing away the gimcrack pine bridge between their island and the shore. Then a surge uprooted their moldy cabin and left it teetering on its spongy sills. Poe had been too drunk to notice. She waded fifteen feet to the shore and never looked back.

But that's the trouble. Others may never look back, but Grace already knows she remembers every day of her life, brown trout in a rock pool, strands of hair in a brush, the expressions of girls peeing at school, books on a shelf, stains on a sheet, damned near everything. Nobody knows she remembers. And when she tells herself she remembers, she answers, I'm left-handed. As if that had something to do with it. Maybe it does. But if it does she didn't learn anything about it from the computer in the Phoenicia Library. Nobody would believe it. And if she proved it she'd just prove she's a freak, which she already knows.

When you remember everything, you know how much people lie. Well, it's not so much lying as confabulating. It's like Lego, there isn't just one combination that works, is there? And that's what counts, what works, a contraption that works. So nobody's ever going to feel okay around Grace, nobody with what they call emotional intelligence, because nobody swallows a lie deadpan, they just pretend they do. Our lives are contraptions and sometimes, splat, we fall off and land face down in the truth.

And if you're going to remember everything you have to decide how to build your library, because you don't have a basement deep enough to hide the images and thoughts, and you will never run out of room. So what will your library look like? It will look like your life. Maybe that's why Oscar Wilde said we pretty much have the faces we deserve by the time we're forty.

She's okay leaving Poe to six-point bucks, largemouth bass and cheap whiskey. But dead is safer. Some people are gnats and motes. They pester the corner of your eye, you have to bawl to wash them out. Grace never got Poe Torrance into focus. He wouldn't be looked at head-on. She doesn't remember crying. But now she knows how to get him out of her eye. This blind sax man here in front of her is going to rinse her eyes with his steep and mournful riffs. She smiles her loony, jack-o-lantern grin to think that unlike her mother Sally, who hid her tips under a rock in the woods to escape the valley, she'd left with pocket change and thumbed her way on eighteen-wheelers to the city. This sax man's notes are better than Spiderman's webs. She can ride them through keyholes and windows. She can soar above the spotty sycamores and piss on wrong 'uns, as Sally called them.

I need some enemies, but what if I'm not cut out for them? Who can you be without them? God has enemies. What about mine? I had Poe, but I deserve a better enemy. I had Heather Romanelli on the basketball team, but I nailed her into that shiny floor. Where are my enemies? I'm serious. I gotta get some. A serious person has enemies. I'm a serious person now, sixteen going on thirty.

The blind man picks a five-dollar bill out of his sax case and hands it to her. What does this tell her? He has the radar, she has the presence. It tells her she's not the invisible type. She feels seen. Not my legs, not cagers' peeks at my crotch, not my pointies, but me and whoever the hell I'm gonna be.

No, you earned it, she tells him.

Yeah, but today you need it, girl. And I need you to come back and keep drawing, 'cause people like to watch us. They like watching you listening t'me, you get that, doncha, girl?

How d'you know I'm drawing? How d'you know I'm a girl? How d'you know who's watching?

You a tall, skinny gal. I see the way we all see, but we scared to admit we see like that. I'm not as blind as most of the people who listen t'me. But you know that, doncha? You got eyes back of your head, and we both know why, don't we? Everybody got eyes all over you, girl, but they don't know how many you got on them, do they?

I wish I could show you.

I bet you do. I feel your ether, I smell your heart.

Whuddha they smell like?

Lilac and New York Bay at 4 a.m. I got your job for you, your profession. Make everything you draw for me. I'll know it. I'll always know it. That green-eyed gal is making pictures for me. I know you a green-eyed gal, ya know how I know it? Easy swimmin', thas how. Tide goin' out. Dark eyes, tide comin' in, oh yeah, didn't know that, didja? Out, way out, gal, I know that 'bout ya, you goin' way out. You lived you whole life to come here today, thas the way life is. We all get to have this day, this one day, and most of us don't even know it. And there you are knowin' it, sittin' in front of me knowin' it. You drawin' it, thas how much you know it, gal. Thas a whole lot 'a knowin'.

What's your name?

Can't have it. Not now. It'd just get in the way 'cause we're mostly not our names. Fact is we're mostly not what people think we is. But I got a name for you, gal. Oh yeah, I'm gonna make you some mad sax for it. Your name be Boudica, B-o-u-d-i-c-a. Killed a bunch of Roman soldiers and bankers. You go, Boudica, that be your secret name from now on. You go to the library and read all 'bout her and in your New York Bay heart don't ever call yourself nothin' else. Thas why you here, thas why you found me in this Union Square Park, to hear that name. You hear everythin' y'ever gonna hear from this here sax, but d'you want it? Boudica, she don't ever forget a thing she hear, not one damn thing, and nothing she ever see gonna look the same again. Lissen t'me, lean over here, you gonna change every damn thing you look at. We all do, but you gotta take responsibility for it, thas the trick. And when you do the world says, Oh my, I can trust that Boudica, I'll give her all kinds of things, ooh yeah! 'Cause that gal, she cop to what she see.

And with that he let rip Blind Lemon Jefferson's *Bleeding Gums.*

Remembers everything she hears, how'd he get that right? Nobody else ever got it. Boudica dreams of girls like her who remember everything. What do they do? How do they live? Over and over in her head she outlines them, colors them, dances with them, but they never speak, they never sing. One girl has electric hands that shock Boudica, another smells like fresh hay. No boys. Just sisters, silent sisters.

***

You put away pieces of yourself, then you pretend you forgot where you put them, not necessarily a bad thing. After a while you don't know who the hell you are. Again, not necessarily a bad thing. Maybe you start thinking you are who you say you are instead of who you know you are. You start acting like you don't know as much as you know because it's what you're supposed to do to get along. That's why Boudica got out. She doesn't want to pretend she forgot where she put herself. She doesn't want to get along. Get along with who, for what?

Sitting cross-legged in front of the blind sax man she knows every day of her life was a stepping stone to him, here, like crossing a kill barefoot and not once slipping on the moss.

My name is Boudica, I'm going way out, I don't forget anything, everything I see I change, and fuck the Huntersville School District, they didn't tell me that. Sally and Poe never had anything to do with me, maybe their silly asses didn't have anything to do with anything. Sally got out, but she left me with that goddam copperhead, faster than a rattler and meaner. She remembers the day a rattler wrapped its tail around her leg while she was standing in the Arendskill fishing. They always said rattlers don't swim. Forgot to tell that one. You ever try to scare a copperhead off? That's what Poe was like, like her memories, just keeps coming.

She looks up at the golden top of the Con Edison Building and gets dizzy. Find out who this Boudica is.

***

Tomorrow's a bucket of light. The Queen pulls her by the arm out of her mihrab. Boudica scurries off to pee in another shaft of light. Her pee glistens like champagne. Then she follows The Queen to a crushed-rock incline that rises to a cross street on the West Side. Manhattan is a city of sides, main sides, B-sides. You can lean against them. You can hide under them. You can groove in them. You can disappear in their canyons. Manhattan lends invisibility to you if you need it, but it can jerk it back and reveal you as crazy as you are.

The Tompkins Square Library reveals Boudica, queen of the Iceni, to Grace. The Romans flogged her and raped her daughters. Their bankers called in Iceni loans. Boudica exacted an awful price, destroying the Ninth Legion and sacking Roman strongholds. Adjusting her eyes to the sunlight outside the library an electric current twists Grace's lips as she remembers how she left Poe, remembers down to the cracks in the floor, the bugs on the wall.

They recover the tunnel queen's borrowed D'Agostino shopping cart from a ratty lot. Then they start the royal progress, collecting and selling cans and bottles, scavenging for food. They're over on Tenth Avenue under the abandoned el when it comes to her, a children's book about Vikings in England she found in a cardboard box of fifty-cent books in front of the Phoenicia library. She and The Queen have bounded out of their dragon ship and are ravaging the East Anglian countryside, she and Brynhildr, the Viking shield maiden. She'll have to fit Boudica into this picture later. Actually, an Iceni queen doesn't fit either, but for now Vikings will do, they're so operatic. At the traffic light at Gansevoort Street The Queen looks down on her protégé—Grace herself is five-feet-eleven—and Grace informs the light, I'm happy. Grace has never said I'm happy. The Queen grabs her arm and pulls her back out of the path of a yellow cab. Happy don't mean getting yourself laid out. She looks up at The Queen and shrugs quizzically. What can I say? I'm happy.

Learning from a mute giant and a blind sax man suits her. Teachers have too much to say. They grind their own axes. They don't listen. If they listened kids would learn more because each kid has a patented way of learning. The Queen has four do's: drink lots of water, pee as often as possible, brush your teeth like crazy and wash your hands every chance you get. This means being wily. Peeing is territorial. The city is designed to prevent you from peeing. Water is life. Let it go through you. It doesn't belong to you. Clean teeth let you look at the world straight. Pee like the Catskills to stay healthy. The creek in you is always rising, God knows what you're going to wash up. You can be the creek or you can be its debris.

Poe, assuming he didn't drown, would not report her missing. He would not report anything, authority being deadlier to him than a Mount Tremper rattler. The Catskill school would go through the motions. But the bottom line is she's as gone as she wants to be. Fuck school, fuck the GED, fuck them all for never giving a damn about anything but my looks. No, I take that back. I miss Mrs. Witte. She showed me how to draw, how to paint. I miss her. I need a new Lois Witte.

And Lois Witte hears, because on the ninth day, after washing in a gush of rain water in Freedom Tunnel, they find a mess of art supplies in a trash can on Eleventh Street in East Village. Stretchers, abandoned canvases, paints, half-used sketchpads, charcoals, pencils, crayons, acrylics—wishbones of somebody's despair. This wasn't a rich neighborhood, wasn't some successful artist celebrated on Madison Avenue getting rid of et cetera. No, this was somebody's defeat.

The two tall women stand over the bin like Druid seeresses. Boudica's face starts to glow. Shadows cross her high cheekbones. She looks up at The Queen. This, this, she says, holding up an eight-by-ten-inch sketchpad, is Excalibur, Brynhldr. This is Arthur's sword. If The Queen knows what Boudica is talking about she doesn't show it, but she's prepared to approve anything this giftchild does. She knew right off that Grace knew the difference between words and sound. If you listen to the city it talks to you. It listens. Its granite and schist are like a baroque harpsichord that turns anything—running water, bus farts, horns, sirens, babble—into music, and all you have to do is shut your mouth. And this girl knows it, so when she opens her mouth, listen, muthafuckah.

Why had no one in Greene County discovered that? Except maybe Lois Witte, who guided Grace's hand with her own and then let it go as if launching a paper plane or blowing a kiss. Lois had even cared enough to see Grace was naturally inclined to minute brushwork, and so had taught her how to use her pinkie to steady her hand when painting miniatures, how to shape her brushes. She had taken Grace to nearby Woodstock to visit galleries and even a few artists' studios.

***

Jean-Luc Plamondon knows Gabriel wouldn't have sung in Mohammed's ear if he hadn't been vetting Mohammed, deciding whether he had ears to hear the Qu'ran. Jean-Luc starts tracking The Queen and her acolyte from the moment he spots them on the west side of Union Square. Our lives are landfills of people we're supposed to pick but pass up. He owes his entire life, his good fortune, to a mother, Jeanne, who knew he was born knowing this and refused to be alarmed because she'd given birth to a child who never cried and tracked everyone like an osprey. If you rub certain moments out of your eye you fumble your life. Jean-Luc isn't a fumbler. In the baseball of life he's a shortstop.

They enter Union Square at Broadway and Seventeenth. The Queen nudges Grace and then pokes into trash barrels. Propelled by The Queen, Grace walks straight to the blind jazz sax man, pulls a sketchpad out of her belt behind her like a samurai drawing his katana and plunks down cross-legged in front of him on the octagonal paving stones. Forget visible means, this is her work. She does this as if she'd done it for a lifetime, she does it with a sniper's focus.

Jean-Luc reties his long sunburst hair and posts himself behind a spooky sycamore. From the moment he first sees Grace's rapt obeisance to Blind Hoxie he knows his life is veering left. It's just one of those things you know, like the moment you know that no matter what you do or don't do or say or don't say, your father is never going to like you and all his patrician protestations to the contrary stink. And you're never going to like him, you being that Jean-Luc fellow to whom I'm bound by some accident, a kind of congenital twin. But fortunately for you the family money is Jeanne's.

Jean-Luc doesn't want Grace, not that way, but he wants to be around her. It's a distinction that confuses a lot of people, but Jean-Luc has always kept it from being a knot. If you need someone without their needing you and they shed their light on you it's a gift far better than a lay or a relationship. What can you say of light? It's not negotiable. It's not formal. Grace burns through sycamore. Nothing occludes her glow. Put her glow like this, How many artists compare to Vermeer?

He knows she's aware of being watched, such a one would have to be, and he knows she doesn't read him as a danger, this girl who clearly senses the worms in the earth and can follow the gaze of squirrels. When you want to be around someone the earth wobbles on its axis, the apocalypse approaches and you call it something else in spite of your best instincts. He can see at a distance that this girl is the kind of girl you fall over towards as if the ground is collapsing. It's not falling in love, he knows better than that, but in celestial mechanics it passes for a monkey wrench. In New York City you encounter heart-stoppers on every block, it's part of the city's allure, but you don't encounter people very often who short out the currents of ordinary existence. It's not their beauty or their charm, it's something far more elemental. Their bullshit detectors aren't passive, they buzz and singe the usual shitters. Jean-Luc isn't smitten, he's scared, and he unerringly heads for whatever scares him.

The ubiquitous looks of models plastered on bus stops, eatchaheartout looks, remind him of Grace only because she's never going to give anyone that look. She's never going to wear fuck-me heels and glance sidelong for the game of it. And when you know that about someone you have to ask yourself why you know, why it matters. Alexander the Great, for all his beauty and charisma, must have had that don't-fuck-with-me look and probably the first person to notice it was his father Philip. The future turns on your either wanting to see Grace in fuck-me heels or being glad you won't. There's no compromise, and of the places in which you could get stuck, if you were Jean-Luc, this is the worst, because it's both irrelevant and apocalyptic.

**

So what's your deal? I mean, I feel you on the back of my neck, but I'm not getting the creeps, so what's your deal?

She gets up in one clean motion and walks over to him so fast he can't put himself together to slide away.

I don't know what you're talking about. Yeah, I can say that, but that's not me. Could I buy you a coffee or something? I mean, I'm wondering how you got to be someone who can't be jerked around. I like it. I like Blind Hoxie. You know that's his name, right? I see you drawing him. I think he knows it, just like you felt me looking at you.

This, this is it, what she came to New York for, the thing nobody ever cops to, except maybe here. This is it, copping to what we get about each other instead of building whole societies on the pretense of what we don't get.

So about that coffee, could you afford a latté? Maybe a croissant?

Coffee? I said coffee?

Yeah, that's what I heard.

No smilers, these two. Grace's cobalt gaze makes his feet sweat—your move, pal. Jean-Luc has one of those graven faces that could not have been made with a sculptor's thumbs. It had to have been chiseled while the sculptor held his breath, like a diamond-cutter striking that one crucial blow. But the corners of his straight, thin lips curl up wryly.

And a croissant, yeah.

So when you're not staring at underage butt cracks in a park, whuddya do?

Jean-Luc has a gift for knowing what to do next or knowing what not to do. He heads west and says nothing. His stride is long. He's six-feet-four and lopes. He wants Grace to come along but he'll take it in stride if she doesn't, and she knows it. She does one of the things she does best, she keeps her mouth shut.

In a manic Starbucks people make way for Jean-Luc and the baristas pay attention. He looks like a dauphin, not that anybody knows what that is. Nobody jerks him around by making him repeat an order, you know, the way underpaid salespeople get over on you.

One hot choc grande no whip and one large latté and plain croissant. Grace notices he stuffs two dollars' worth of noblesse in the plastic tip box. Is everybody supposed to do that?

Nobody cadges a table at Starbucks around noon, but Jean-Luc with his balletic grace finds one.

My name is Jean-Luc Plamondon. You need a job?

Sometimes you blow tomorrow away like dandelion seed

because you don't say the right thing, you look at the ceiling, you look the wrong way. But the seeds go somewhere. Perpetua fortuna—the people who have it don't need any epiphanies about it. Maybe it's presence, maybe it's prescience, maybe it's their respect for the moment.

My name is Grace Torrance. I live in Freedom Tunnel. Why wouldja offer me a job?

(She has it, perpetua fortuna. Didn't know that, didja girl?)

That's funny, Grace, you live in just about the one place where there's art I can't move. I'm an art preparator. I think this is a two-latté conversation. Oh, and yeah, for future reference, I don't answer why questions.

He gets up and orders another hot chocolate and latté. Then on an inspiration he orders a Tuscan turkey focaccia for Grace and another one to take out to her large friend.

Is Grace your real name or did you make it up for me?

You don't look like that, ya know, the sort of person people make up names for. Grace is my moniker, you can't have my real name. I don't give it away. Wasn't that Blind Hoxie's schtick? She feels the blind man's presence in the park behind her and works hard deep inside herself to take in his words. Jean-Luc has disrupted this process and yet he seems part of it, too. After all, he's shared the blind man's name.

That's smart, Grace, because when you do give away your real name it loses its power. That's why you should never show anybody what you're working on, never. A good teacher will respect that, a bad one will flunk you, but who gives a shit, you've already flunked him?

He's flying way ahead of her, and she's loving it. Her lips wander off into a pleased sideways smile, not unlike the actress Lena Headey's. She thinks of Lois Witte. This guy takes her seriously. Maybe he wants something she won't want to give, maybe she will want to, but right now this is good, a good give-a-damn conversation. Jean-Luc is handsome. No, he's beautiful, and she wants to tell herself he's not her type, but she doesn't know what her type is, hell, she's not even sure she has a type.

But he's beautiful and she's not bad, and people are looking, and it feels so far from Arendskill. Fuck Arendskill.

***

The curators and registrars in a museum or a gallery know what they want. Where to hang a painting or put a sculpture, what to say about it, that sort of thing, but I'm the person who gets it done. I pack and unpack art. I move it. I install it. I repair the walls, strip and polish the floors, plaster the holes and paint them... I wire paintings. I get them framed or reframed. I put up rolling walls and fake walls. I even install lighting. I'm the do-everything-else guy. When you look at a piece of art I'm the guy who put it there, and I take it away, too. I store it. I'm invisible. I'm supposed to be. That's why I'm thin. This is not a fat guy's work. In the art world I'm a knife slicing through butter. You're not supposed to see me but you'd be in a pile of shit without me. Lemme see your hands. Yeah, you got the hands. Can't have stubby hands in this business. Disappearing is elegant, we have to be elegant.

Elegant... her loony smile is the remembrance of a world where elegance was a brown trout and little else. She'd like to be elegant and disappear.

Catskill High School becomes a speck. Every word plinks her like warm rain. Can you imagine a job like that? Who ever heard of a job like that? Invisible, can you dig it? That's... she rubs the throbbing in her chest.

Could I wear overalls?

White. You have to watch out for buckles. You don't want anything to catch on the paintings or poke them, nothing to ding the sculpture or the edges of walls. No rings, nothing like that, no metal, nothing sharp except your head and your eye. No punk, no goth, gotta look righteous 'cause we're dealing with The Man. The Man wants to strut his stuff. We're not like the maid, we're more like a hired assassin.

You teach me?

I'm doing it. Thing is, Grace, you never stop learning. There's always some better way to do something, some better tape, some new lighting idea, something all the time. You gotta start loving hardware stores, gewgaws, gimcracks. You gotta go to galleries and see the way the artists and gallery people do things. If it looks like you've seen it before, don't waste your time on it. That's how you spend your time when you're not working, because you're always working. You have to see everything and be open to everything. The minute you think you know how to do something you're history. You just do your best until a better idea occurs to you or you see somebody do something better. This is not a business for smart asses. We're all waiting for the light. That's why there is darkness. The universe is very new and the light from each star takes a long time to get here. We're all waiting. And you never know how a certain star is going to affect you. But... how's your sandwich?

Fuck the sandwich, what was he going to say?

He was going to say, But never wait to hear from anybody. It's not like waiting for light. Fuck them. Never wait for anybody. She can see that. If she hadn't kept up he'd have just kept walking. For the second time in her life she's happy. Delirious. A new name, people to take her seriously, a job even, a serious job, not flipping burgers or dodging customers in Best Buy.

But?

Then he says it: But never wait for anybody.

Not even you?

Nobody. How old are you, really?

He didn't like his own question. It was manipulative.

Is anything? Worth waiting for?

Did that come out of her mouth? He wants to kiss her. But? Why? He's not attracted to her, not that way. Some people are born to be strangers. How do they taste? That's why he wants to kiss her, to know.

I'm sixteen.

Anybody looking for you?

Nobody ever looks for me, not gonna start now.

Jean-Luc has been looking for her.

Thing is, I come with The Queen.

93

The queen?

Yeah, the big blonde. She doesn't talk. But she comes with me.

You bargaining with me?

No, John, I'm just saying I can't leave her. It's the way it is.

It's Zhahn, not John. I'm Zhahn-Luk. It's French. She as strong as she looks?

Zhahn?

Right. Zhahn-Luk. The Luc goes with it. Brynhilde goes with you, Luc goes with me. Okay?

Is it okay? I mean, you're giving us jobs?

Freedom Tunnel's not going to work. You're young, so I'm guessing you can learn to live somewhere else, but sometimes people like Brynhilde there get used to being outside and they can't live inside anymore. They gotta be outside because inside does a job on them. You gotta work that out, Grace. I don't know what to tell you. Here's my card. Work it out. I'll give you jobs and figure out where you can live, but you gotta work it out. Maybe she's like Blind Hoxie, he can't play inside. It doesn't matter how good the acoustics are, he can't play inside. You could give him Carnegie Hall, he doesn't want it. Some people call it crazy, but I think it's a question of who's crazy. Gotta go. Spying on you has cost me some money today, maybe even a client. But it was worth it. Hope I hear from you.

Zhahn-Luk is out the door and gone before she puts her turkey focaccia down. Knife through butter. About the queen? Good sandwich. Will there be other days like this? Do I deserve other days like this? Why not? I'm tough, but I'm not mean. I never wished anybody dirt except him—his name slipped away like a leaf in the Arendskill, him, how am I gonna wash him out of other guys? Out of Jean-Luc. Well, him never offered me anything, sure didn't offer to show me how to be invisible, I had to do that myself, and it didn't work.

***

Something about him. About him slicing through buildings, sliding off people like rain, putting words where they ought to be, like brushstrokes, persuades Grace to check him out, something she's used to doing. No sense taking anybody seriously just because they show up. Some teachers are so full of shit all you have to do is study how full of shit they are.

She used to see cards on cork boards in eateries, but nobody ever handed her one. She looks over Jean-Luc's card the next day, a Saturday, and checks the subway map to South Third Street in Brooklyn. It's just north of Washington Plaza near the east foot of the Williamsburg Bridge. His card has a handful of sugar cubes spilling out onto his name. Turns out he lives in an old Domino's Sugar factory. The Queen is over in Tompkins Square Park collecting cans and bottles in the street and pocketing stale sandwiches from Bachinsky's deli. Dunno if I can get The Queen to work for Jean-Luc, too soon to say. Besides, Boudica hasn't made up my mind yet.

Jean-Luc and Grace can make themselves two-dimensional like sheet glass or metal. But Grace can peel her presence off people. They don't feel her watching them. She used to work at erasing her shadow from things. Some people have an aura like thickets of bullbrier. People get torn up in it or have to skirt it. But Grace can call hers in. An artist in Lexington once told her she had a gold and purple aura. She had been disappointed. She would have liked a white aura. Maybe he was wrong.

But here's Jean-Luc and his alien eyes. They're both disappeareds, she and Jean-Luc. Somebody can swipe a cellphone, but nobody can lift your penchant for fading out. They wouldn't know what to take. Maybe it would be better to have Jean-Luc's ghost eyes, maybe even his pale hair. But they're both cards under a door, light prizing a crack, wind under a sill, chill or warm, and mostly gone. He's gone before arriving, and in his line of work this is a good thing. People she likes disappear or disappear her, just fall out of her orbit, or she falls out of theirs. No room at school ever seemed to recognize her one day to the next, but her basketball coach always acted glad to see her because he needed her crazy, spinning jump shot. She knew trees better than classmates and liked them more. Nothing's ever where she put it, and she likes that, gaming the order of things.

***

Jean-Luc checks things out. Check him out. They both know when not to poke copperheads. A copperhead's a viper. Having grown up half on the Upper East Side and half in Paris he's seen plenty of them, but not by the littorals of creeks. Jean-Luc and Grace move like shadows on granite buildings and most people are mica-blind to them. They know that being striking and chimerical is rare, but wearing the gift lightly is something else. Being gone, the practice of being gone is preemptive. That's how they wear their gift; they look as if they will be gone, and if they're in your crosshairs you're sick with love and you shake.

The Atlantic's briny breath is close. It tricks the sycamores to bud. She stands sipping a burned coffee and watching Jean-Luc's sugar factory. Judging by the apartment number on his card, he lives on the top floor. The big louvered windows are open. After an hour and ten minutes he breaks out on roller blades. He's wearing a backpack. He jumps the curb and races towards a falafel cart. Roller blades are hot. Grace needs some.

What does a man who feels watched do? He is, after all, being invaded. Since it's Blind Hoxie's admirer—Jean-Luc is almost certain—he'll do nothing to nettle her privacy. It's not a matter of honor, it's defying the hypocrisy of pretending we don't know things we do and do know things we don't. He thinks for a second of turning away from the steamy cart and bowing towards her like an Elizabethan courtier, but his instinct tells him this might piss her off. She's not to be trifled with, and neither is he. The Purple Mountains conspired over his head to send him this zany. He and Brynhilde share this feeling.

***

So, if you become what you want to become, will you ever have to become anything again? If the answer is the sun that warms his back as he walks to the park this might be the day of never having to go home, day of unknowing. It feels like a pat on the back, this hot sun. It's going to thrill Central Park with lasers. It propels him like a nursemaid as he looks for his favorite bench. In Manhattan the sun propels you up and down certain streets and blinds you to doubt. This is one of the many reasons artists come.

You eat that shit? The nitrites'll kill you. My name is Grace Torrents, T-O-R-R-E-N-T-S .

And I look like I care?

She shrugs and skates out towards Fifth Avenue.

Hey!

She turns and skates back.

Listen, Miss Torrents, I'm an old man and if I want to eat a dirty-water dog I'm gonna eat a dirty-water dog, and I could tell you a few things about names, too. But you don't have one of those instantly likeable faces, you know. Does anybody like your face, Miss T-O-R-R-E-N-T-S?

It's kinda stony. Enjoy your nitrites.

The pasha sizes up the czar's envoy. He keeps on looking as he walks from the halal-and-kosher hot dog wagon to a nearby bench. This envoy's head should be sent in a leather sack to an enemy. You like impertinence, you old devil, stop complaining. That face'll stop lovers midstream; they'll never come across. That's why you like Manhattan, faces like stars in their heavens.

To plop down on a park bench as hard as she does requires a posh tush, which Grace noticeably lacks. But this high pile of humanoid stuff losing its shape in carnival ways intrigues her. His cane has a silver dog's head, or is it a wolf's? Maybe he cracks people's heads with it. Neither of them is sure there'll be another word between them. Neither of them cares. Skaters pass, whiny toddlers, snitty mommies, surly nannies, mimes dressed as statues, street artists, muggers, bombers.

So you gonna tell my stony face something or we just sit here and listen to ourselves breathe?

I notice you pull your hair back behind your ears. Is that because you like to hear things or because it accentuates your eyes?

Accentuate, that's a Lois Witte word. Mister Nitrite here might be worth a listen.

It's so my ears don't itch.

Ah! Well, humor doesn't suit your face, Miss T-O-R-R-E-N-T-S, but I can tell that with you it's fatal. You don't care if I laugh, you just like to make yourself laugh deep down where nobody sees. Am I right? Where do you laugh, Miss Torrents?

No egg or soup on your tie, you probably live around here. I don't laugh at anybody.

Gets personal right away. Where do I laugh? Like I'm gonna tell him.

Very astute. You have the acumen of a pimp. I think I'll tell you something. Whuddya wanna hear? You gonna tell me your name?

What a pedestrian question. You can do much better. If I could live without a name I would. A name is how they jerk you around. That's why they call it a handle. Do you know who they are? Hmm, I think perhaps you do. I'd like to live without a shadow or a mirror image. I'd like to count the leaves on locust trees, the stars. I have other ambitions, but I don't know you well enough to tell you. I don't know anybody well enough to tell them anything, especially not graceless torrents. Where did you learn a word like acumen?

Grace-less Tor-rents? She herons her neck around to the uptown position and stares at him, one of those girls whose mouth is shaped for a certain fixed startledness which fashion photographers usually translate as drop-dead gorgeous stupidity.

Mooks like you... that's all that comes to mind, Mister Nameless.

Excellent. A big, tottering mook leaning on a stick. Yes, I like that. I think I'm going to fart. A nice celebratory fart. A mook is entitled, don't you think?

Grace sticks her forefinger in her mouth and then holds it up.

Okay, the wind's from the south, go ahead. Grace Torrance is the name I was born with. I always thought it Torrents after what it does in the Arendskill Valley. Think of me as the former Grace T-o-r-r-e-n-t-s of Arendskill because if it wasn't for them

I wouldn't be here. The torrents. They feed New York City with its famous water. That's where I got the idea: why shouldn't I join those torrents down to the city? Ya don't like my face?

Trust it, yes, like it, not so much. We probably shouldn't trust the faces we like. All these benches are empty. Why are we sitting here? Oh, and by the way, did you know the city is full of people who can't think or talk as fast as you?

Torrents shrugs. Torrents splits.

***

He's been sitting on this bench since 10:30, not just today but for weeks. Ten-thirty is when he's supposed to be there, when Shrugs-and-Splits is supposed to reappear. He has no idea why. How quickly she'd had enough of him. How edgy their encounter had been. He has no idea why he's supposed to be here. But he's had a lot of bad ideas in his time and now no idea seems like a good idea. But being in the right place at the right time is his vocation.

The buses fart operatically. Grande dames with brown rats on leashes scuttle by. Girls Grace's age walk over the cobbles three abreast fixing to mow down old men and gawky boys. The shadows of clouds race across buildings, scurrying djinni.

He stretches out his legs on the cobbled street and shuts his eyes. As a boy he wasn't foolish about girls. As a man he savors women from a distance. They have always seemed superior to men. More commonsensical. The men with whom he once did business were always throwing dazzling women at him, but he chose his own and not often. Why in his old age he waits for Grace Torrents on a park bench he can't say. Doesn't matter. It's like the difference between dealing with Sendero Luminoso, whom he likes, and the IRA, whom he doesn't.

***

The muthafuckah, I'm gonna kill him.

Grace wheels out of the park and falls on him like an Ontario Clipper, plopping down with a jolt, her wheels spinning in the air.

This muthafuckah, Girlie, he needs killing?

Girlie? Who the fuck said you could call me girlie? What're you, some kind of molester?

You're molesting me. Did you know there's a cab driver in Washington named Molester T. Foxworthy? It's painted on the door of his cab.

Her wild eyes pinwheel in the sun, turbines catching the winds of this and that and whomever. Her bronze hair is tied back to one side—thoughtfully, he thought.

You look like you need molesting, you know that? And yeah, the muthafuckah needs killing.

It's muthafuckah, Miss Torrents. And you've chosen the right person to molest, Miss Torrents. Perhaps you have good instincts that do not entirely complement your bad manners. Now let me ask you, is it the killing you want to enjoy or the muthafuckah's being dead? The former is like candy, but the latter is wealth. Killing and death have quite distinct rewards, according to whom they belong.

Are you gonna buy me a dog or what?

I thought you didn't like nitrites?

So buy me a falafel.

Why should I buy you anything, Miss Torrents?

Ya wanna hear my story or not? I mean yer sittin' on a park bench ogling girls. I'm a girl, I gotta story. Oh, I get it, you like blondes.

Are you in training to be one of those East Side bitches who mow old men down with strollers and fuck delivery boys to spite their predatory and derivative husbands who invent financial instruments like roadside bombs?

I'm their worst nightmare. I wouldn't fuck them or their husbands without a full-body condom.

Mmm, no, you wouldn't. I can see that. My name is Wulftan Ertugay. You can call me Wulftan for short. I do not ogle girls, I anoint them with adoration. I wish them every good thing. You have a story?

I'll call you Wulfie.

It wouldn't get you a falafel. What do you do besides worry

old men and make foolish noises about killing a species called the muthafuckah? Killing people is serious business. If you breathe a word about it, you're not serious.

And you know this because....

It's a long story. I'm not sure you deserve to hear it. You may think of me as an enabler. Temporarily, until I decide whether I like you thinking about me at all. Yours may not be the sort of mind I want to inhabit.

Yeah, like this is under your control.

The leaves show their wan undersides. The wind carries away the moment. Wulftan rises unsteadily. The hot dog wagon rolls further uptown with Wulftan in pursuit. The Girl Who Wants To Kill The Muthafuckah looks away.

***

Beryl Sutphen dreams about finding a coral snake nestled in her undies drawer. She likes the coral against the black. She starts locking the drawer with one of those antique keys, the kind you see on charm bracelets. Then the snake worms into an ear and whispers to her about an old hat box. She rummages in her boxes and finds a four-by-five-inch miniature painting in a distressed green wood frame.

A tall black-haired woman in the painting regards Beryl, just as the yellow-eyed snake did in her dream. The woman stands on the near side of a pond laced by aspens. A girl of perhaps nine holds her hand. She peers into the woman's face. The eerie miniature painting vibrates with expectancy. The air in it quivers like one of Corot's aspens.

Beryl doesn't recognize the pale woman with blue light playing around her face, but she knows the girl. Beryl was nine the year her innocence was looted by the managing shithead of her father's law firm. This tall woman is not her bipolar mother. She's a queen or a goddess, Beryl's guardian. So where was she when Douglas F. Hereward III Esq. gave Beryl the special responsibility of keeping her family intact by keeping "their" secret?

Where had the fierce-eyed queen been then, when a little ferocity was needed?

Days pass before Beryl asks herself the more obvious question of how this gem got into a hatbox stuffed with lingerie she'd never worn. Who knew how she looked at nine? Where is that pond? Had her mother owned this painting? Why doesn't she remember it? There were many paintings handed down in the Sutphen family, but she doesn't remember this one.

She paces around her apartment at Two Sutton Place, holding the little painting at arm's length, studying it, then clutching it to her breast. Finally she sits on the white Russian sleigh seat at the foot of their bed. She grips its griffin arms, hers and the wife beater's. No, the griffins are hers alone. She winces, remembering her lord and master whipped her only nine nights ago, whipped her with a little leather belt from her own closet. Something about her hygiene. Her scent. She had been playing with herself, the jerk-off said. Wanker, Beryl, the British say wanker. Who gives a shit what the British say? But yes, he's a wanker. Now she can't even lie in the sleigh and dream of whisking over snowlands listening to the bells. The wanker has stolen her dreams, echoing the Hereward's sin.

You can see a therapist for a long time and never tell her anything like this. After all, you present yourself as a grownup, don't you? But if you don't tell her, what's the use of seeing her? You play the game, that's all. It's a gaming society, right? Doesn't asshole call investing casino? The investors take their beating, Beryl takes hers. Asshole wins. This is a society invented for assholes, maintained for them. Women are their harem, half the world, and the other half their slaves.

Well, he's winning until her underwear gives up his nemesis. A delicious chill slithers up her groin to her head, and not even her favorite floppy blue Nordic cap can keep her warm. The colder she feels the more dangerous. This is a blue-lit snow cave. The griffins are winged, Beryl, remember that. She is ashamed in front of the noble griffins. The griffins winced when she was whipped, not for the beating but for her passivity.

In that painting, is that Beryl before or after the managing predator set her up for these beatings? She doesn't remember wearing such a dress. But it's a dress she would have liked to wear. Now a Pre-Raphaelite picture from her adolescence comes to her, she knows who this queen is. It is Boudica, queen of the Iceni. Fearless Boudica. Vengeful Boudica. She takes the painting to her dressing table. She looks at herself, then at Boudica. A smile slowly widens her mouth. She drops her nightgown and twists herself around to examine the welts on her behind. Boudica will give Asshole more than the S&P to worry about.

I am going shopping Mees Beryl, Rocio the maid announces. She has been vacationing for two weeks and this is her first day back. Rocio sees things crumbling. She sees cracks everywhere, edifices falling in slow motion. She tries not to look at the naked queen in the Nordic cap.

⁂

Beryl makes everyone whole by making Douglas Hereward's secret hers. That's the job of abused children, to make everyone else feel okay. To call shit gold. But that Beryl didn't have a coral snake in her undies and that Beryl wasn't staring into Boudica's eyes. That Beryl was familiar to everyone but herself. This Beryl knows a few things about herself. And she knows somebody else does too, somebody out there in the grandeur of what could happen.

Make it snappy, Beryl, we're running late, Winton Xenophon Payne calls from their cavernous Arabescato Vagli marble bathroom, compared to which restrooms are a relief.

Beryl winks at Boudica. Whooshing deodorant under her arms, she peers into the grandiose bathroom and says, Did I mention, Win, that if you ever touch me again I'll cut your balls off while you sleep? They make very sharp ceramic knives out of zirconium oxide these days. Scuba divers and bomb disposal people use them. I saw some just the other day at Conran's.

C'mon, Beryl, this is an important engagement. We need these clients.

Well, I hope they like eunuchs who can hit High C.

Very funny. I'm not fucking around here, Beryl.

She looks in the mirror. I'm-not-fucking-around, she mugs

103

v-e-r-y slowly. Then she pulls out the drawer and picks up the miniature again. She smiles at the queen, puts her back in the drawer, and gives the towhead in the mirror a big smiling evil finger. Because the image in the mirror is the old Beryl Sutphen who is going out to entertain clients with WXP. And they had better act nice or they'll meet the new Beryl Sutphen.

She makes a final check in the mirror. Wassup, Doo?

**

Well, I think they're on board, Beryl. Thanks for holding your end up. Guess you're feeling good. You've been smiling all night and one thing you're not is a smiler. Should I be worried?

Say what? Besides his balls, what should The Payne worry about? She's enjoying the suspense. How could she have married someone too stupid to get it? Well, of course, she married the very kind of guy she'd been keeping her secret for, her father's kind of guy, a Hereward sort of guy. Oh yeah, you should be worried, especially since you forget who's got the gelt. Their real wealth, Nana Elaine's, the wealth everybody's eye is on, comes to her next year. Yes, all in all, WXP has more than six-foot Iceni queens to worry about. He's been wearing his red-plumed helmet too tight and it has affected his memory. Should you be worried? What good would it do you?

It's a lot to take in when you can't sit comfortably or sleep on your back. But she enjoys her welts. She's been sitting too long on her breathtaking ass. The welts are a blue-chip investment in the future. WXP thinks he's opened another door to fun and games, and so he has. But he isn't going to like them. Beryl Payne is about to get on with nine-year-old Beryl Sutphen's life.

**

Morton Street Preparators? Did you have anyone at Winton Payne's house at Number Two Sutton Place yesterday? Yes, I know you don't have access, but I thought someone might have let you in. Okay, tell me the names of the people who have worked here for you, will you? No, you can call me tomorrow with them. Thank you.

I don't like the way you look, Mrs. Payne.

Wulftan Ertugay holds the elevator door for her with his cane.

That's because I'm looking like a Beryl this morning, Wulftan. Perhaps you don't like beryls.

You are most certainly a gem, but beryls I don't know. Do they look like garnets?

Beryls abound under Manhattan Island, Wulftan. We're an isle of beryls. They're pale green, garnets are reddish. You could call Manhattan Beryl Isle.

I think I'll call it Beryl's Isle from now on. Trouble is coming, Mrs. Payne.

Must I be Mrs. Payne, Wulftan? Why is that?

Formality is required when trouble is coming. Are you sure you're not a blood diamond?

Wars are not fought over me, not yet. And you're right, trouble is coming. An insurgency. You know about them, don't you, Wulftan? You know a lot about them.

They're my bread and butter, or should I say my jam? Someday we must have a chat about how you happen to know this. I thought I was merely an eccentric old blob to you.

Nobody is merely to me, Wulftan. Who would have thought la-di-da Mrs. Payne actually gives a damn? By the way, did you see some people in my apartment yesterday. Morton Preparators?

Yes, I saw Miss Grace Torrance. And I have never thought of you as la-di-da.

What does a Miss Grace Torrance look like, Wulftan?

Tall, copper hair, crazy eyes. Very strange girl. You couldn't miss her. I met her in the park. I tried to talk to her yesterday, but she just pointed at me like a, like an assassin. Upsetting, because she once molested me for a hot dog when we met in the park.

Molested him for a hot dog? A smile quickens Beryl's thin lips. A crazy girl molesting Wulftan Ertugay in Central Park. It would be lovely to fall asleep thinking about that. Now, who would have thought Poe Torrance's losing something had anything in common with Beryl Sutphen's welts or Winston X. Payne's future as a eunuch or... Jean-Luc Plamondon's business? Who would have thought it but an arms merchant whose success depends on sensing how things come together in the air? Satellite is such a primitive device when you have your senses, all of them, especially the ones society has urged you to hock. An arms merchant would have to collect art because he knows with artists how to apprehend them when events meet in the air.

Wulftan Ertugay is a believer in the Butterfly Effect. A revolution might have failed or succeeded depending on an encounter in Central Park between an old Spahi and a loopy girl, and in this sense no one ever knows what's going on while at the same time everything impacts everything else. The little things that go unnoticed made Wulftan his fortune and enabled him to do what governments can't do because they move like foot soldiers in armor.

***

He goes back almost every day hoping to see her. He keeps turning over what he wishes he'd said, like a boy who botches a brush with a pretty girl and replays it the right way in his head, sometimes for the rest of his life.

My name is Wulftan, meaning wolf power. I want you to know that. I want you to know about my mother Ursula, my father Alp not so much. He was a sanitation engineer, a.k.a. garbage man, in Cologne. You don't need to know about him. You would have liked Ursula.

But it's too late. He'll never see the girl again. That's what happens when your brain sinks to your shoes, squish, squish.

And then there she is in the lobby, handling a big painting and acting like somebody sent her to shut his mouth. Yes, that girl needs to shut his mouth. He knows that. And she will, she'll do it, because she's not a trivial shit-eater. In fact, I don't know what she is, do you? You, Wulftan, d'you know? Maybe Izet the Bosnian Muslim resistance fighter sent her to kill Wulftan for selling RPG-7s to the Serbs, maybe the Serbs sent her for selling AK-47s to the Bosnians. I'd hate to die with cheap mustard on my face.

How odd for an old man to want to redo an adolescent

moment. But where is the chagrin? An old man should feel chagrin for acting like a young fool. But it's better than dead liturgy, isn't it? I want to ask her about that pointed finger, that cocked thumb. I don't want to ask the Shining Path or any one of the boring Saudi princes I've dealt with, or Mike Bloomberg or Paul Krugman, but I want to ask Grace Torrents who the sonofabitch is who needs killing. I want to ask her on rollerblades, with mustard on my face and sauerkraut in my lap, not because I'm hot for the girl but because in her presence cut flowers last another day. How do I know this? Look at me, wilting but for my expectations in the park. No, she said, muthafuckah, didn't she? Not sonofabitch. That goes without saying.

***

Beryl sees his mind has wandered from their simple encounter in the hallway. He's distracted. He needs a painting to focus him. She strokes his sleeve lightly before leaving the elevator in the lobby to go out into the sparkle of Beryl's Isle. Her gesture restores him to himself.

Mr. Ertugay is talking to himself. He's getting old, Luis Rios the doorman tells the manager, Pat Noonan.

When you fuck with that old man it rains body parts in Surabaya, Pat says.

Pat is odd, too, Luis thinks. Where the hell is Surabaya? There are people in Belfast who think Pat is as dangerous as Wulftan Ertugay. But Luis merely thinks Pat is odd. You have to get used to dealing with Irishmen if you're an immigrant. They belong to the gatekeeper class, not being brown. But Pat looks like if you try to handle him he'll do something you won't like. So Luis just listens, not knowing that Pat likes eccentrics, even if they're just doormen.

You can't come in the front, Luis tells Morton Street Art Preparators. You didn't reserve the freight elevator, you have to reserve the freight elevator. There's a list. Luis doesn't get that art isn't furniture and ordinary rules don't apply to demigods and sometimes not their minions either. He also hasn't observed who has Pat's license to break the rules.

We're not carrying these paintings through the side, too many angles and sharp edges. Jean-Luc Plamondon looks down on Luis Rios from a great height. His long blond hair falls like sunlight on the dapper door captain. Jean-Luc looks around for Patrick. Patrick appears from the recesses of the grand old building.

Mister Ertugay's masterpieces! Howya doin', Jean-Luc?

Patrick, my man, tell me how it's comin' down.

Comin' down hard, Jean-Luc, hard.

Wulftan Ertugay is the major shareholder. His penthouse is practically a museum.

Luis doesn't have a clue what these gringos are talking about. He's not going to prevail. The gringos belong to the same club. Luis speaks English but not this English with its mystery messages, its vernacular magic. This is coded English, like rapper jive, only franchised to tall whites.

***

WXP, like Wulftan Ertugay, is a major shareholder, kind of a commodore to an admiral. He doesn't have Wulftan's impeccable taste in art or anything like Wulftan's concealed wealth, but he's obvious about what he has. Rules are for the hoi-polloi. He tips cheap. If Beryl knew how cheap she'd be ashamed. Wulftan, on the other hand, has the staff in his employ.

Londonderry is behind Patrick, but MI-6 has better connections in the States than he has. The pooh-bahs of Sutton Place value his resourcefulness and discretion. Patrick is one of those Irishmen who avoids the drink like an article of faith, knowing it's a British ally. He also avoids it for the company it keeps. Patrick can recite Yeats for every occasion, but if you ask him he can't tell you anybody who knows this, and that's fine with him. He likes to tell his Irish friends, just to piss them off, that come Saint Patrick's Day he looks for the nearest Italian bistro. The New York Irish and their romantic notions of The Boys, always passing the hat for them, sicken him.

Patrick sees Boudica at Sutton Two, as he calls it, all the time, usually with The Queen. They repair and paint walls, hang and re-hang paintings, sometimes just for a big party. He syncs with them. They share a knowledge of who not to fuck with, starting with the three of them. Patrick sees something about Boudica she doesn't see about herself, because he shares it with her. She thinks sex is okay but she doesn't know about gender. Women leave and men intrude. Patrick and Boudica think sex is an itch and gender a pain. Imposing as the girl looks, he wouldn't think of making a pass, but he knows the city is full of gobshites who would. She's a fellow bomber if ever there was one, but he's out of the business and she's into something else, which the paint that haunts her fingers is trying to tell him.

I wouldn't like her for a sister, I wouldn't like her for a lay, what would I like her for, what do I like her for?

And Patrick Noonan likes Boo a lot.

I like her because she's tall, but not because she's hot, because she's not, she's cool. No, she's cold like snow melting and sucking the warmth out of the air, and deep down inside she has that blue light that sometimes leaks into her eyes, that blue light in snow. Jaysus, Patrick, ya'd think ya were in love with the girl. Yer in love with her, arncha? Not. So what are you in with her? A kind of conspiracy, is it, of people who think anything that makes insiders makes outsiders and ought to be blown up?

It's the question Boo raises and doesn't give a damn about.

***

When he spots her wheeling a fifty-by-sixty painting through the lobby on a dolly, Wulftan emits a looking-for-love call. Like a mourning dove. She stops, balances the Reinhardt with her right hand, and shoots him with her left forefinger. That's their history, shot dead on the marble floor. Luis sees nothing, which is why he's the doorman. Pat sees what he sees, not an old lecher, not a wily girl, but a knot both of them are working. A terrorist's mind is a casbah of twisty turns. The girl's gesture reminds Pat that Mr. Wulftan Ertugay knows a great deal about weapons. That was no Glock the girl pointed, it was a .22, an assassin's weapon. If a Tommy saw Boo on a Londonderry corner he'd ask her for her papers. A smart Tommy, that is. And maybe an even smarter Tommy would pass on by. But what about a girl who fucks with Mister Ertugay? Is it like Beryl Sutphen fucking with Pat, teasing him when he says Sutton Two by saying Sutton Hoo? Hoo? he asks one day. Hoo, Patrick, not Who. Hear that whuh? she says in his ear.

Gotta watch her, gotta watch out, can't risk this gig. And then one day she knocks on his office door and when he opens it she plunks down a big, splashy coffee table book on his desk. It's all about Sutton Hoo, the famous Anglo-Saxon archeological dig.

It wasn't just flirting, was it? This high-tone babe, this knockout, wants him to know about Sutton Hoo, wants him to understand her play on words, wants him... gotta watch it, but whatever it is, it doesn't make him think of the drink, and whatever excitement, whatever enticement doesn't make him think of the drink is worth thinking about. But not on Sutton Hoo's time.

***

Grace points her left forefinger at Wulftan, not a bang-your-dead finger, but a you're-in-my-crosshairs finger, the thumb straight up. Wulftan takes note. So does Patrick. Wulftan's poor dead body is going to rise off that cold, polished floor. A cocked thumb would mean something else. She doesn't smile or nod. Pat gives her a wassup-wichu-you look and she looks back as if she had his papers in her pocket. May I see your papers, please? many a Tommy had said. An Irishman can make himself a lot more comfortable in New York than a Salvadoran or an Arab, but an IRA bomber is a creature apart, welcome in the saloons Patrick hates and always in somebody's crosshairs.

Pat likes this old man. He's far and away the best tipper in the building, grateful for every little help, thoughtful to a fault, and always eager to engage staff in talk. He knows Wulftan gives money anonymously to any of the help in need, even the lowliest porter. He hopes the old man is on guard. He should be. They've lived their lives vigilantly, both of them. They know the world is full of authorities and they're all bad. He doesn't like Boudica shooting the old arms merchant. The girl would make a good operative, but she'd end up too soon in a Londonderry dump.

110

But Wulftan takes the girl's finger under advisement, as lawyers say. Just as a wise Roman consul would have taken Queen Boudica's gaze. What's he done to deserve this mock assassination? It wasn't The Finger, to be sure. But it wasn't hey-howya-doin' either. Had he lost another piece of himself, this time to a tetchy girl?

***

Sometimes I find pieces of myself in drawers with mouse turds, in shoes that have gotten too small for me, in moldy boxes crawling with silverfish. I know the epithelials are there, but I mean pieces of my sensibility, my software. You'd be surprised how much of yourself you can do without. Some days people pass through me, I can walk faster on one leg or get by without my head. I never lose a hat, but I leave my head everywhere. I always get it back. Nobody wants it. It's full of dead bystanders, arms and legs, crazed militias, scowling ayatollahs, bullet-headed ethnic cleansers. If I leave it in a restaurant, old people go home and die, the cook strangles his girlfriend, that sort of thing. What did I leave with this girl? What's her game? I like her. Does she think she's got my number, that I'm a dirty old lecher and she wants me to know she knows? She must be smarter than that. Who's not a dirty old something, even the young? I'd like to know, but I don't know how much I'd like to know.

Look at this! Look at what goes on in this snotty lobby. A girl pops me, a retired bomber interrogates her, an old man wonders how to wind things up. Look! You're not going soft, are you? You're going to do something important, like screwing an old widow out of her money or stabbing a partner in the back, something you can be proud of, something you can wear to the University Club. Something that Payne-in-the-Ass does every day. I hate his fucking guts. I like Slobodan Milosevic more. I like Tamil Tigers, Zapatistas and Al Qaeda nutcases more than you. So Wulftan, what're ya doin' here among the cocksuckers and their camp-guard wifeys? Tell us, Wulftan, do ya belong here? Here, there, anywhere. Where do ya belong, Wulftan Ertugay? Isn't this a helluva way to die? Any way is a helluva way and who the hell are you? I'm the man who negotiated with Slobodan and Al-Zawahiri, that creepy suck-up. I'm—anybody you want me to be, anybody I want to be. What kind of arms do you want? I have scruples, I don't sell to drug cartels. I have principles. What do they think I do at The Frick when I give them a Masaccio? Do they care?

* * *

You're listening to Wulftan's hobby. He loves New York argot in all its iterations, Irish, Yiddish, Russian, Sicilian, you name it, and he talks to himself in whichever of these argots seems appropriate at the moment. Actually, you're listening to the two Wulftans, the one with the name and the other nameless one. The one with the name was originally supposed to be the sensible one, the comforting one, keeping a frightened boy company, wisely counseling him. But lately they've been arguing. Put yourself in the shoes of a priest who's gotten used to preaching to the choir, then one day the chorister whose face he likes best gives him the finger. Some days the priest laughs, some days he has trouble swallowing.

He glances at Patrick Noonan. Pat shakes his head once to the left, just once. Forget about it, Mr. Ertugay, young girls are as witless as they're dangerous. But Patrick, too, is disquieted by the girl's gesture. Patrick was drawn to perverse girls when he was young. But in time he came to realize that life in a nitro kitchen isn't for mature men.

But perverse doesn't describe Grace T-o-r-r-e-n-ts, does it? Not volatile either. She's... Patrick reaches far back... she's fey. Ya've stayed alive, now, Patrick, by knowing what people are, and this girl is, how would ya put it, this girl is likely not to show up in a mirror some day, and likely to be right behind ya when she comes to mind. And ya've stayed alive by knowing what's behind ya, what doesn't fit, who doesn't fit.

* * *

Patrick has his own way of staying alive, but it's not mine, not Wulftan Ertugay's. Patrick lives in the interstices of things.

I live in the knowledge that grandees have their uses. Saddam Hussein rolled out the red carpet for me in Basra. I spoke to him about Sinbad setting out from Basra in search of the roc and the thug humored me because he needed river-crossing pontoons. I dipped green Cohibas in Calvados with Che Guevara and we talked about poetry. He was civilized.

Wulftan Ertugay is surrounded by people he likes in a familiar place, but he can't make heads or tails of it. Forget it, Mr. Ertugay, oh yes, Mr. Ertugay is going to forget it, soon. But Mr. Ertugay wants to do his forgetting in style. Winton Payne isn't worth talking to, but Patrick Noonan is, and Rad Estevez, the handyman, is. And it would be fun to hear more spitfire responses from Grace Torrents. Who wants to die listening to the usual bullshit?

***

Do you paint, Jean-Luc?

Beryl isn't short, but Jean-Luc has to stoop to look into her eyes. She's never seen him in anything but a milky way of paint splotches on white coveralls.

You name the museum or gallery, I've probably painted it.

Paintings, Jean-Luc, I mean paintings, your own.

I mess around.

Why don't I believe you?

Why don't you?

This entrepreneur thing you do, this gregarious shtick, I don't believe it. You're only alive at night in your loft somewhere, painting. I think you live on coffee and don't communicate very well with Houston. I think you paint on rollerblades and skate between three or four easels at a time. I think you're eldritch, Jean-Luc, and eldritch is good. I think maybe you're a vampire, Jean-Luc. In my mind I'm spelling it with a y. I don't think you'd like my blood. It would grow things in you that you wouldn't like. A conscience maybe. You wouldn't like one of those, would you, Jean-Luc? Can you make great art without a conscience, Jean-Luc? Next year, if I still like you, I'll pay you a hefty commission for an answer.

What a bitch! You have to have platinum looks to pull this

113

shit, this goddamn psychic autopsy, cutting me up on a steel table and pretending we're flirting. I'll bet that hologram of a husband slaps her around.

Jean-Luc doesn't like people who think they have your number. B-movie actors playing Nazi interrogators. Their attitude gets cops killed. Until today he liked Beryl Sutphen Payne. He always figured her for better than her mouth. He always figured the mouth was an antidote to Payne. He figured her for a wild animal that gets into a house and can't find its way out. Nobody's ever going to know her by her mouth. It's just going to talk her down the wrong street. She's one of those people you have to do something about. I'll bet she was a wonderful child. I can see the child in her when she shuts her mouth. This is a chrysalis I'm looking at. Something is emerging. Maybe I'm the first to see it. Maybe she's going to shut her mouth, and this is a work-up. I like her with her mouth shut. It's not the voice. Her voice is nice, soft, respectful. It's her smile. It doesn't know when to relent. She just pastes it on and there it is. I like her face in repose. I'll bet the kid hardly ever smiled. This smile is for Winton X. Ghoul & Associates.

Jean-Luc isn't the kind of person who ducks somebody in anger. He doesn't know what to do about this new Beryl. He doesn't even know if he's sad or mad. Where does she get off suddenly knowing me and thinking I drink people's blood? What do I do with this high-paying in-my-face client? He unfastens the pearl buttons of her white silk blouse. Slowly, troubled, trouble she likes.

He should be troubled, and I should tell him I know a vampyre wouldn't be.

She looks down at his long fingers, the ones she has accused of making art, and decides she's pleased to be his art, the art of this lightning-struck and animated Lembruck. But how pleased? She has wounded someone she likes seeing, someone she admires. What's this? Nine-year-old Beryl grown up mean? This is nine-year-old Beryl's buttons he's undoing.

Long time coming, this, this what? Beryl Sutphen doesn't

fit into Jean-Luc's scheme of things, but neither does Grace Torrents. Trey Godling fits, and that's what feels so wrong about it. It, what is this it?

Jean-Luc, you are beautiful and smart and charming and everything a girl could wish before her 18th birthday. And you're not a vampyre. No, you're thoughtful. But people are not whims, so put your charm away and send me that tall girl who works for you. I want to rearrange some paintings for a reception and I need help.

Here I am, Beryl, at your service.

Mmm, are you at anybody's service, Jean-Luc? Or is this an improvisation? That's what you do, isn't it, Jean-Luc, improvise? Send the girl.

Beryl turns to a window and re-buttons her blouse. Patrick Noonan comes to mind, sitting on his battered swivel chair with his long legs on his desk. I want to own or at least borrow what that man has seen.

***

When Boo arrives the next day she finds Beryl's apartment door open. A girl of the last century might have called yoo-hoo. A 21st Century girl might call Yo or H'lo. But Boo stands in the doorway, knowing perfectly well the doorman called up to get Beryl's permission to send her up.

Some of the two women's affinities buzz. Beryl spots Boo and walks over to her quickly and quietly. No effusive There you are! or, Grace, how nice to see you!

I want this girl for something and I don't have to know for what, do I?

Let's sit for a minute. I'll tell you what's up. You'll need the wall paint in the foyer closet, some putty, a blow dryer, stuff like that. I just want you to move a few paintings. But first…

Beryl unwraps the little painting in the green frame. What's this? I mean, I see what it's about, I think I do. But why? I would have paid you for it, you know.

Then it wouldn't be any good. It wouldn't do you any good. It wouldn't do me any good.

It is good, it's very good, Boo. Is that what they call you? I heard Jean-Luc call you that. But I know your name is Grace Torrance. You're not going to tell me, are you?

Boo shakes her head slightly.

You like me, is that it?

I see things, I feel things. Sometimes. Not with everybody. Then I paint them, what I see.

Did you see a snake and not put it in the painting, Boo? Would you tell me?

A little red snake?

Beryl's hand palsied. Uh huh.

Have you ever done anything like this before?

Lots.

Always with rich people you meet working for Jean-Luc?

No, usually not so rich people.

How d'you meet them? D'you break into their homes?

Yeah, I meet them or I kind of spy on them and then I break in. It's easy. You can always shine on some guy to let you in downstairs, and most apartments have crappy locks.

And then what do you?

I walk around, I go through their things, I sit, make myself tea or coffee, see what they eat, what they wear, go through their photographs, lie on their beds. I paint in the air. I sing, sort of. Different kinds of sounds in my throat, my mouth, my nose. The whole place hums. Then I go home and paint.

You don't make sketches, you don't take notes?

No, it's not like that. I never forget anything. I remember every single thing. It's because I'm left-handed—that's what a lady psychic told me. I remember where things are in books. I remember things other people don't even see. Something just comes to me. Sometimes. Or not. Then, if I make a painting, I bring it back and I hide it somewhere special. Sometimes maybe they'll find it right away, sometimes maybe not for months. I don't care. I don't care if they never find it. It does things. It changes things.

You remember everything, every day of your life? You remember smells? Colors? How can you stand it?

Yeah. See, the hairs on your body are like towers, transmitters, and your body is like a country, and each hair sends signals. And then the hairs on my body get the signals, and that's how I know who you are and if I want to make a painting for you. I can't stand it. That's why I paint. Whatever I paint doesn't bother me anymore.

And these are particular hairs?

Yeah.

This is very spooky, Boo. Very erotic. Which particular hairs of my body spoke to which particular hairs of your body?

Boo isn't one to look out windows or search walls to evade a challenge. You really want me to answer this, lady? Her look tickles Beryl's eye, her nether parts itch.

Boo would consider this flirting if she cared about flirting. Beryl Sutphen had always struck her as someone else, someone Boo was supposed to touch in a lockpick's way. She feathers the side of Beryl's face with the back of her left hand.

Beryl takes her hand. My dear left hand, she whispers. There doesn't seem to be anything left to do, any way to break the spell. She puts Boo's hand on her hip, holds the girl's face in her hands and kisses her, softly at first, then searchingly and long. She doesn't want to send Boo along to do her chores. She doesn't want to sit and socialize. She doesn't want to step away. Boo doesn't want anything. Not Beryl's money or her body or even her friendship. She just wants to be here, near. They want to breathe each other. Everything else strikes Beryl as vulgar.

But this costs you money, Boo. And it takes a lot of time. And you could get caught and go to jail, go to jail for breaking in and giving somebody something. That's so odd. But it's not, is it? It's not funny to you. You have to do it, don't you? I love this, Boo. I love your painting, I love what you do. I admire you. I want to be you. You don't want to be me, do you? You don't care about money. I think I know what you're doing, what you care about, and then when I think about it I don't know. You're like something I think I saw in the corner of my eye.

I know what you mean. That's how it is for me. I don't know

either, but I want to do it. It's like my life depends on it. Once in a while there's someone I have to do something for, so if I have to climb a fire escape I do it. I saw this blind sax player in the park and I had to draw him, and he gave me five dollars and my name, Boudica. But I didn't make him a painting, not because he couldn't see it. Something else. He didn't need it. And when I saw you I saw you didn't belong here or anywhere. And I had to paint someplace where you belong.

And you know all the colors of my underthings and my books and my papers. Do you remember them?

I remember everything. Your things are like a garden, I remember the flowers and the scents. It's not like I got something on you. I don't get over on people.

No, you don't, Boo. Neither do I. But I've let them get over on me. I have an idea. Would you like to be my sister, Boo?

Uh-huh. Boo moves towards the foyer closet for the paint.

Beryl calls after her. Does Jean-Luc know? Does he know you have this career and it's not the one he thinks he gave you, Boo? Does he know?

No. The Queen doesn't know either. She thinks I'm keeping the paintings. She thinks they come out of my head.

But they do come out of your head, Boo.

No, they come from what I see, from everything I see, from the first time I see the person to when I see their apartments. I'm not making the paintings up.

Don't you trust Jean-Luc, Boo?

I'm gonna set up the fans and open the windows and doors, Mrs. Payne.

Of course you are. Beryl feels as if she could sit in her living room with this girl for a lifetime, a feeling not unlike Wulftan Ertugay's. She has never communicated with anyone, not even Nana Elaine, so directly. And Grace has never before felt herself toppling towards someone as if the floor couldn't be trusted. Beryl strikes Grace as ready to catch her if she falls.

What's going to become of you, Boo? What do you call me? Mrs. Payne? Call me Beryl, that's my name. The whole island of Manhattan is full of beryl. What's going to become of you, Boo?

What's going to become of you, Beryl? That's the answer she hears as she begins pulling cans of paint from the closet, and then an image of Patrick Noonan arrives. Grace hurts with a new inchoate impulse, and Beryl senses it and comes into the foyer, leaning on an archway.

Who do you see, Boo? Who do you see now? You need to break in and make another painting, Boo. Can I count on you to do that? I know you do, I know it's just what you'd do if I disappeared this moment. Am I right? Is that how it works? Something happens and then you know what to do. You see a photograph, a scarf, a half-eaten sandwich, a toothbrush in a glass, something, maybe even soiled underwear. You're not a voyeur. You know what that is, right? You're not a spy. No, this is espionage. Divine espionage. You're a daemon, or a very dangerous angel. Not a sappy, churchy one. I get you, don't I, Boo?

And what's it worth to Goldie here to get me? Is this like sitting down in front of Blind Hoxie? Is this the moment? And if I can't sit right here and make her a new one, can I paint it in her mind? Here's what I know about you, Goldie. When I look away from you I see ten algae-green bursts in the shape of an anchor. That's what you get for staring at the sun, ten green bursts in the shape of an anchor descending to the bottom of something. Leave me alone, I should say. Let me sit here in the closet and make this painting. She'd do it, she'd leave me alone.

The thought is better, more thrilling than the bank shot she suddenly knows she can make. Can I paint it in her mind? Not on paper, not on canvas, but in her mind.

Beryl stares at her, her lips parted, waiting. The girl, her sister, has seen something, someone. She's doing something. Let the phone not ring. Let there be no sirens or horns, no shifting of the blocs of light.

Tall, slightly stooped as if weary, his bleached blue eyes resting wherever they fall as if he had a lifetime to talk to you, his sandy hair disheveled as if a lover had just tousled it. Patrick Noonan, the super, now what has he to do with what may become of them, Boo and Beryl? The super.

Remind me to see if Wulftan will tell me anything about Pat. I know they're fond of each other. Who will remind me? Nine-year-old Beryl? Boo? Boo is reminding her. Beryl's parted lips come together as they must to form the letter P. Boo nods, then turns back to her work in the closet, organizing paint cans and putty.

When Boo stands and turns from her work in the closet Beryl is right behind her. They stand not more than a foot apart, feel each other's heat, bask in each other's scent, and the absent Patrick Noonan stands between them.

***

Boo's long body seems to float on her uplifted heels, Mercury's winged heels, Beryl thinks. Her red hair is pulled off to her right and tied with a black ribbon, exposing a fragile neck that reminds Beryl of Jeanne Hébuterne, the painter Modigliani's young mistress. She is pulling paint cans and brushes from the roomy closet. Beryl sits watching on a white empire sofa.

Only one inevitable person has ever inhabited Beryl's world, Nana Elaine. But now she can't imagine a world without this feral girl. She and Nana had chatted amiably about faeries and their haunts. The only reason Beryl could be drawn into the country was the possibility of its yielding a faerie.

Boo?

The girl turns slightly but doesn't face Beryl.

Do you ever watch yourself in a mirror?

I know what I look like.

Of course you do. I mean, do you ever fear you won't be there?

Now leave the words hanging in the air, Beryl. Don't bother this girl with words. She doesn't like them. Don't mention the teenage girls who check themselves out in store windows, making sure they're still there. Don't mention it.

I'm not there, Beryl. Isn't that what you mean?

Now, Beryl. A few words, the right words, and then shut up again, because this girl is feral and always will be. This girl is maybe not a girl at all.

See, I don't imagine you walking when I'm not looking, Boo. I think you fly, not operatically, like a bird, but just a few inches off the ground, and I think when you turn a corner you go far away and you won't be there if I run and look.

That's enough, a bit too much, Beryl. Words sting this girl. Even loving ones. Love is a funny word to come to mind here, isn't it, Beryl? No, it's not. I love this creature, and I don't know why, and I know I don't need to know.

Boo rises in one sweet gesture, like a Picasso line, and stands in front of Beryl just as if there hadn't been five yards to cross. She fingers Beryl's tow hair from her left ear and kisses her ear, more like a soundless sentence than a kiss. The warmth of her kiss fills Beryl's head and a scent rises from Boo's faint breasts that fills her with eagerness.

Faeries and vampires have no mirror image, Nana said. What does faerie's breath do in the blood? There is no Nana to ask.

What does faerie's breath do in the blood, Boo?

The right corner of Boo's mouth quivers. I don't know, Beryl, but I like what I don't know much more than what I know.

Now if I say what Mrs. Winton Payne would say—What a preternatural teen-ager you are, dear—this moment will dry up and blow away and me with it, not because it would be like looking a gift horse in the mouth, but because it would desecrate the way we've found each other, the way we've chosen to deal with each other. Could that be true of Mr. Ertugay and his friend, Patrick? My friends, Wulftan and Patrick? I must grow up this instant, not tonight, not tomorrow. I've run out of time.

She gets up. A bit taller than Boo, she finds the girl's wild cowlick set slightly back from the left side of her forehead and buries her lips in it. They embrace. For a long time, swaying a bit like one of Manhattan's many towers.

***

121

Trey is maybe ten years older than me. His hands have a tremor. I want to reach over and quiet them. I can tell he's ill.

When you look like an Anglo nobody questions the source of your wealth. Money is the Anglos' IV drip, at least on the Upper East Side. Everyone thinks they know where Jewish money comes from. But when you don't quite look like an Anglo or a Jew, and you're not surrounded by men who look like refrigerators, you're suspect. That's me. Suspect. I might be a deposed sultan or raja, but people who know there are millions of Turks around the world might just think I'm a Turk, which I am. How many Turks live alone in seventeen-room penthouses on Sutton Place? Who gives a damn? All Trey Godling knows is I'm not an Anglo, and that's either a tragedy or the good fortune of Anglos, depending on how you look at it. I know who he is, but I forget how. I'm sharp. In fact, that may be what he thinks of me, sharp as in dodgy.

Wulftan Ertugay, Mr. Godling, I say. He motions for me to sit on "his" bench, since the others are occupied.

Do we know each other?

What crap. Put the other guy at a disadvantage.

No, but I know of you, Mr. Godling. Please call me Wulftan.

Umpf, he says. Isn't Wulftan a German name?

Yes, it is. My mother was German.

We sit. He's uncomfortable. We're all born uncomfortable, but he seems never to have managed to make himself at home. Perhaps he wasn't at home. The only discomfort I enjoy is that of bankers, lawyers and diplomats. I'm worried about his palsied hand. I don't need him to like me. I'm not prepared to like him. But one never knows, which is the only reason life is worth living.

A very liberated mommy or a very willful child. Get us some chili dogs, will you?

Trey looks younger when I get back, dribbling con carne on the pigeon-blue cobbles.

They're terrible for you, but I love them, he says.

He lives in a tony townhouse a little farther south on Sutton, one of the few to survive the girdered hard-ons. Schooners and cutters used to dock there. It has a copper mansard roof that I admire for its patina, especially when the evening sun burnishes it. We've had a nodding acquaintance. I've always thought he regards me as one of those arrivistes who in an earlier and better New York would have been consigned to the West Side. He's had some pretty la-di-da limousine soirées. But most of the time his house suggests he's in southern France. I never figured to bump into him in Central Park. I'm sure he has his own park somewhere. And I wouldn't have made him for an artist either. No, he looks like somebody's son, simmered in inheritance.

Sometimes the benches in Central Park are crowded and there's no refuge from the stroller Nazis and the smart-phone zombies. It's that kind of day, preternaturally sunny. He makes room and motions me to sit down rather like a king to his jester. I guess I'm looking a bit frantic. Two old men sit there for a moment and then he says, I like your face. Neither of us know what else to say, so he sends me for hot dogs.

I'm not usually at a loss for words. His voice is boyish, enthused. On the phone I suppose you'd never take him for an old man. I sit staring at the French tricolor snapping in a brisk breeze from the second floor of the consulate at 934 Fifth Avenue and after a while the damnedest words come out of my mouth.

I've tried to paint, I say, but I can't.

I'm sorry, he says.

I believe him. He is sorry. And when he says no more I realize it's because he has good manners.

You paint, don't you? I've seen you toting canvases about.

How do you know they're not someone else's?

I'm a collector. You only handle your own paintings that way, like hyperactive children. No reverence—just, I want to say, parenthood.

His blue eyes stare at me amusedly through their rheum.

Mmm... I have a story to tell you. Do you want to hear

my story? You'll have to keep me company. A week, a month, maybe a year.

Do you know who Boudica was, Woolf-tan?

I nod. Yes, that's my name, and you've got it right. Sort of.

Queen of the Iceni, gave the Romans fits.

Mmm, but who would name a girl Boudica today?

I'll tell you about Boudica. But I warn you, I may die before the end, I may even die before I get her whole story out of her. And then where'll you be? That's how it is. We never get the whole story, you see. We have to die before we do. We die and nobody gives a damn how concerned we were about this and that. But if you live long enough pieces of the story you've buried rise up from the dead and wake you up in the middle of the night. What would we do with the whole story? Would we be sadder to leave or happier? Did you know that's what fireflies and swamp gases are about? Departed souls telling you now they know, now they know what you wanted to tell them, what you didn't want them to know, what they didn't want to know. Signals. Bogs are about more than methane.

He's getting the story about Boudica, the dead Iceni queen? What is this? What game is he playing? But who would've thought this toff thinks of signaling fireflies and swamp lights and bogs? I sit there trying to recalibrate my opinion of him, but the words that come out of my mouth are unworthy of what he'd said. Here we are surrounded by these unbankable treasures in their skull cases, acting as if they hardly matter.

The whole story makes for a bad painting, Woolf-tan. An artist must know when to stop. Not much makes me angry anymore, but an art dealer who tells me a painting is unfinished or anatomically incorrect, well, I'd like to beat him down his elevator shaft.

He loves this. He sifts the city through his teeth. Yes, of course, why didn't I know that? The whole story is a gaucherie, isn't it? Why do you think Cézanne left parts of his canvases bare? Why do you think de Chirico loved empty piazzas? Have you noticed, it's always Sunday afternoon in his paintings. You should be listening to Chris Botti trumpeting Nessun Dorma when you look at those piazzas.

He looks at me to see if I know my Puccini.

I smile. I know just what he means. Nothing is as lonely as Sunday afternoon in the city, and Botti plays Nessun Dorma as if he loves de Chirico. I wonder if he does.

I'm so charmed by Trey Godling, even by his condescending toying with my name—it's a familiar WASP trick—that for a moment—until just this moment—I forget he's pulling a fast one, a particularly dirty fast one, because he knows I know a Boudica who is not an Iceni queen, although she's queen of something. He knows, this old sonofabitch, because we use the same art preparators, and somebody has a big mouth, probably Jean-Luc Plamandon, making time with his connection to me. This is shit, but what else have I got to do? Besides, as usual, I have a powerful secret. Okay, Trey Godling, you think you're playing me, but I'm playing you, which is how I got rich.

You don't know I have a painting to show for your story, an exquisite miniature whose signature you can't read without a jeweler's loupe. The signature says Boudica. And Boudica doesn't know I know who she is. So I'll listen to Grace Torrance's story, Grace Torrents's story. I'll grade you on the telling of it. The only thing you've got on me, you old fox, is that I suspect you know I sit here morning after morning hoping to have another chat with our Iceni queen. I don't want you to know that, but I think you do. Yes, goddammit, I want to hear her story, what do you think I've been sitting here morning after morning for? But not from you. What is this, some kind of arbitrage? I'm entitled to hear the rest of her story, where do you get off horning in? What is this, packaging derivatives for suckers?

I might just lever myself up on my cane and walk off. I've done that kind of thing. But I like this plummy old gent, I do now at least, and what if this is the only way I'm going to hear her story? And there's the pure synchronicity of hearing him mention Grace. Here's what I know about synchronicity: use it, don't poke it. That's how you sell bad things to worse people and get rich. I have a talent for liking unlikely people. I liked Milosevic. But I would have liked him better dead. Maybe that's the way it was with the Germans' dread fascination with Hitler. I feel like pissing from my ears. I nod. Yes, I want to hear. People who like de Chirico's piazzas shouldn't have a grand compulsion to speak. If this man wants to talk it's because he has something to say.

You can misspend your money on all kinds of charities, Trey says. It makes me melancholy to consider them. My few remaining relatives are loathsome. I'm indebted to them: their wishing me dead keeps me alive. Nothing to the whole rotten lot of them, not a penny! He bangs his fist into an open palm. My regime is to wake before dawn, sit by my east window, shut my eyes and let the dawn draw my face. The dawn always uses soft, crumbly charcoals, never a pencil. Then I begin to draw or paint. I work until mid-afternoon and then I stick a sketchpad in my belt and go for a long walk, stopping to sketch architectural details, gargoyles, curbstones, cornices, street scenes, whatever interests me. But I believe in celestial interventions, or satanic, I don't care which. Sometimes a plan pushed through to the end is botched because you should have let something arrest it. That's how paintings are overpainted—the artist lacks respect for what may happen, or not. You have to listen to the celestial mechanics. You have to be willing to be ambushed by inspiration. Caution is for supply sergeants. We always talk about ambush as a bad thing, but for an artist it's a good thing. Unless you're thick.

***

He's dying, and dying to tell me about Boudica. He's like a stray leaf pinwheeling down on a wet watercolor. Artists who have no tolerance for accidents are second-rate. So what does it matter if I have to get to the park by 10:30 to keep him company?

He never picks up where he leaves off. He's like Proust, you have to bear with him to mine the gems. He retraces his steps. He's in love with memory. Thank God he's not dying of Alzheimer's. We eat too many hot dogs, but at our age it doesn't matter, it isn't the hot dogs that are going to kill us.

***

126

Boudica is seriously pissed, Trey announces one morning. She lies to me. I don't like it. She's violent. That's what she lies about. She's telling people she wants to kill the muthafuckah. I'm sure it's me. It's so tawdry and theatrical.

I know about this muthafuckah, I say. I mean I know about her wanting to kill him. She pointed a finger at me recently in my lobby, but she has no reason to be mad at me.

Did he hear me? I know who this muthafuckah is. Does he even notice I know her? Why does he ignore me, as if he knows I know her but discounts it? He doesn't know I know her. What's this? If this were a deal, I'd walk away from it. Is it a deal? This smells like skunk cabbage. If a genocidal Serb general acted like Trey Godling I'd sell him defective RPGs for an exorbitant price.

She hates fingers, Maestro, Trey says—an artist appreciates this—they're busy and sneaky. Beautiful fingers bear special vigilance. Especially hers. She's left-handed but nearly ambidextrous. More about that later. Here's another thing you'll appreciate. Do you like minimalists? Never mind, it doesn't matter. Boudica always knows what not to say and she knows the perfect moment when not to say it. Knowing when to say something isn't half as good, and knowing what to say is for preachers, politicians, talk show hosts and other putzes. Our affairs are managed by putzes, you know that, don't you?

Maestro, me? What's this? You see what I mean about bearing with Proust? Did Proust know what a putz is? Maybe Proust did, but Trey Godling? He grew up at dinner tables where you're supposed to know what to say. Don't bother me with events in Tikrit, I don't care about Waziristan, this is an urgent question. Some men in Trey's position would have figured out I know a lot about putzes. He likes what little he knows too much. He's not deep, but he's fey. What time in his life would I have liked him? As a kid I'm sure he was a prick. Maybe this is his only likeable time, and maybe it's up to me to value it.

I could tell you I love Boudica, but that wouldn't be the half of it, Trey says. Boudica is loose from another dimension. She was knocked loose and picked herself up and made herself at home. Fuck them if they can't take a joke, she tells herself. That's her maxim, Maestro, they being elementals from that other dimension, you know. Boudica is a fellow elemental. I'm staking my life on it. She's a piece of mischief. She was born Grace Torrance and always thought it Torrents because that's what it most often does in the Arendskill Valley, which is probably the most remote part of the Catskills. Dreadful place, the Catskills, morose, mangy. George Washington hated them. Only the best anglers know where Arendskill is. She didn't dislike her name, but a blind saxophonist in Union Square Park told her about Boudica, so she had the name tattooed on her arm by some cokehead in the East Village and started thinking of herself as Boudica. It would be interesting to have a discussion about why she chose that spelling. Another day perhaps. Then last Halloween when she was scrounging around Soho she started calling herself Boo for short. Boo, get it?

I was thrilled to hear all this and mad as hell because she told him and not me.

The Arendskill, a famous trout stream, has a cluttered, ripped flood plain and the Torrance cabin sat only about fifteen feet from the normal creek bed. Grace lived there with her father, Poe. He fished, hunted and cut wood for a living. He messed with me, she told me. He won't fuck around with anybody anymore. I snipped his figs with a pair of scissors. Now, I ask you to savor this, Maestro. How likely is it that poor country girl ever saw a fig? Poe Torrance had to be a profoundly stupid man not to see he was fucking with the wrong girl. And there's this, Maestro: how are you supposed to look when you tell someone you snipped your father's figs?

How did she look?

Trey looks away. Why doesn't he know, if she told him? How did she look when she told him? My meetings with Trey Godling have reached one of those nadirs when the undersides of everything appear, like the undersides of leaves in a breeze, like a slow-moving video lit by lightning.

That's the moment I saw that everything serious Grace has to say turns comical on her face, Trey says. Beauty in a woman can look eerie, especially if she has long eyes. But loony beauty in a woman is rare. You have to have a cowlick or two that no hairdresser can control. You have to have a zany impulse, like shooting an old man with your finger in a posh lobby. You have to have a gap between your two front teeth.

Whoa, Proust! Maybe there was a Grace on your Paris streets, Marcel, but you didn't know her.

Boudica has two, two cowlicks, Maestro, one up front over her left eye and the other on the left side of her crown. Her bronze hair crops up like winter wheat from them. It incites you to make faces at her. But her eyes, large and unwavering, sober you. I like the price this Poe person paid for messing with this nobody's daughter. Eunuch Poe, fuck him. That's his name from now on, because our girl, Maestro, the self-righteous bitch snipped his figs.

And you, goddamit, don't remember how she looked when she told the story! Am I gratified? I don't think so, Proust. Are we talking about an elemental? Yes, I think so. Two old lechers. Is that what we are? We? What I don't have in common with Trey Godling would fill a library.

That's what she told me, Maestro. There was a flash flood when she was sixteen. It cut a whole new branch around the north side of their cabin while they were sleeping. Grace jumped out of bed when she heard the cabin groaning as it tilted towards the creek. The new bank was widening and they were going to be swept away. In a few seconds the floor started breaking open and then the ceiling. A beam knocked Poe out just as he was sitting up in bed trying to clear the liquor fumes out of his head. It pinned him down, and that's when Grace thought of the scissors. Then she grabbed a wild grapevine and pulled herself across the new creek and up the opposite bank. She called the emergency medics for Poe from a phone booth in the hamlet and hitchhiked to Manhattan. For all she knows he bled to death. Vicious vigilante, dangerous as hell.

Are you kidding? That bastard got off easy. What she did should be a tradition. Her mother left that child in his care. She did the work of an avenging angel. I'm not sure you're fit to tell this story, Trey. This is a quintessentially American story. Boudica is an American goddess, not a delinquent. You're too European to get it. I thought I was the European, but I get this story. This story makes reality TV look like Pablum. We should line up to kiss this girl's ass. Instead we suck up to creeps in suits.

That's what I said, I managed to say in my indignation. I want this story, is what I didn't say. I want it for myself. What did Trey Godling do to deserve it? I mean it, what did he do? See, this is what happens in this country. Draft dodgers play war heroes. Anti-Semites make movies about Jesus. I could go on, but I'm thinking about bonking him with my wolf's head.

Trey gets up, sorts his stricken bones, straightens himself as best he can and leaves me sitting there in the bloody pool of what I didn't say. I've thought about it many times. Did he think she enticed the woodsman? The world is an enticement, doesn't mean we should loot it. I was sure I wouldn't see him again. If I did he would look away. That's what his kind does. What do my kind do? Well, that's life's big question, right? It can't be left to a Saint-Gaudens, it must be determined beforehand.

I'm desperate to know what happens to this girl who puts down her bloody scissors and hitchhikes to a new life in a city she's never seen. This girl who plops down one day next to me in the park and announces she's going to kill the muthafuckah. I mean, really, this is muthafuckah central. But unfortunately the muthafuckahs are not all being hunted by a berserk faerie with scissors. I'd like to know exactly where she put those scissors. This teenager is conscious, that's what makes her dangerous. We think unconscious teenagers are dangerous, but a conscious teenaged girl can bring down empires and sometimes has.

**

Wait a minute, would you mind if I interrupt this for a station break? First of all, I don't know whose story this is. Is it

Grace's or mine or Trey Godling's? Isn't she supposed to tell me this story? Remember me, Wulftan Ertugay? Everybody sounds like somebody else, except me. I still sound like me. Is that an accident? What's this Trey person doing telling the girl's story? What does he know? I'm the one who's been sitting on a park bench waiting for her to come back. Every story needs someone like me to sit and wait to hear it. Me, I'm here.

We don't know each other's stories, none of us. We don't know each other, we just pretend we do so we can get away with all kinds of adolescent shit. Everything we think we know is just a label to stick on somebody or something. Yo, Wulftan, doo, chill! Every good story is a lie. Nobody operates according to a plot. When you try to control the plot you don't make the deal. Listen to the story, that's all. See what's up, what the storyteller wants. Isn't that how you got rich, Wulftan, listening to stories? Sure it is. Who says you have to believe it? Damned-fool historians used to say the Athenians at Marathon made a human juggernaut by running a mile or so at the Persians, and that's how they won. Then someone asked, You mean those hoplites ran a mile in all that bronze armor? Give us a break! So there he is, Trey, running in all that armor.

**

Tall. That's what Trey tells me six weeks later when I find him again in the park. I come almost every day, looking for him, hoping he's still alive. Tall, she was tall, almost full grown. Very long fingers. You don't deserve this story, you know, Maestro. I'm entitled to my opinions. I didn't have to tell you a damned thing.

All things are damned. Tell me about the fingers.

They have a life of their own. She's an artist. Did I tell you that? Gifted. Uncanny to have such skill so young.

No, you didn't say that.

Yes, better than me, much better. But I don't think she can handle anything big. The girl likes detail. Mad as Giotto, wants to give mystery a face. She looks at big canvases as a kind of flatulence. Just guessing, of course.

Life is not a horse race, you know. We don't have to be

better and bigger than someone else. Let me tell you something, the Visigoths fought the Saracen invaders on horses that were sometimes eighteen hands high and they were no match for the Arab mares. Do you like that story, Trey?

Yes, yes, I do, Maestro. A big bluey tear wobbles in his left eye. But in America we do, Maestro, we do turn everything into a horse race. That's what America is about, a wretched race, a trumpety war, and in between we don't know what do with ourselves. It's called exceptionalism. The rules don't apply to us, and if they ever do, fuck us. The Native Americans called themselves The People, but that's not enough for us, we have to be the best people. We can't leave anything alone, we have to adjectivize it. We celebrate heroes for their taciturnity, but we're the most adjectival people on earth. The Italians don't compare. We ruin everything with the extra stroke. Nothing we do withstands a black-light examination. This is an awful thought...

He can't think of Wulftan's name.

Maestro, yes, an awful thought, a people whose society shows connivance under black light.

He squints at Wulftan. Not bad for an overgrown brat who's hobnobbed with pirates wielding briefcases all his life. He's made an accommodation with his terrible recognitions. Give him credit for having them.

Isn't that true of all societies?

Well, there's varnish and there's varnish, Maestro. None of us withstands much scrutiny, but it only whets our appetite for hypocrisy.

I don't know at what point Trey became Boudica. Perhaps I imagined it. He wants to become someone before he dies. He hears her voice, her way of speaking, almost every day, so what she says is always fresh in his mind. And yet she doesn't sound like the girl I met in this park. Trey is receding, like the Cheshire Cat. Frail as he is, he seems to appear from nowhere and vanish into crowds as if I'm blind to the particular colors of his clothes. You can watch some people cross Fifth Avenue and walk away, but Trey erases himself. I don't really want to know who he is, the way we don't want to explain how we made a certain painting. I don't trust artists who do a lot of explaining. Or, put another way, I don't like them. They should be like doormen, a Zip-locked guild.

I start squinting at Trey as if I'm having trouble seeing him. If you have to die, fading away from a park bench is a nice way to do it, especially if someone is hanging on to your last word. I think he knows I'm having trouble seeing him. I think he likes the invisibility coming over him. I think he isn't sure he wants to tell the rest of Boo's story. Maybe this greaser next to him doesn't deserve it. I admire this. He's losing the thread of the story. I think he's improvising. Proust goes into great detail as he tries to figure out what he wants to say. It's his charm. It's as if he's not always sure the reader deserves this memory or that.

I call you Proust in my head, you know.

Marcel?

Himself. You've read him?

Three times. It's hard to be the person you want to be, the person you ought to be, when you want something or someone. But if not now, when? Would you like to know my one remaining ambition, Maestro? I want to know what happens to the last oak leaf that is finally blown away in a December gust, precisely what happens to it, how it makes its departure, what it encounters, as I'm encountering you. This is a very high ambition, Maestro. Will it be granted me?

The wind turns another leaf.

***

Trey, wait a minute. I've been gaming you. I know more than you think. I know you're gaming me. I'm waiting to see if you're the muthafuckah she wants to kill, the muthafuckah she mentioned when I first encountered her. You don't need killing. I think we should collaborate. I met her here, just like you. We had the same conversation about hot dogs. She asked me to buy her one, just as you did. I met you because I keep coming back here hoping to see her again. Then I see her one day in the lobby of my building and what does she do, she points her forefinger at me like she's going to shoot me, like I'm the muthafuckah. I'm your greaser, but I don't think I'm her muthafuckah. Either you know I've been waiting for her to appear again or you're just bragging about your liaison with a young girl, inviting me to wonder if you're doing her. I have to tell you—well, no, I don't—all this says much more about you than me. She was like the inside of a tulip to me, a kind of precious air, the kind of scent you're afraid you're never going to be able to place again. So here we are, me wanting to hear about her, wanting to like you, and disliking you because of your wicked game. This is not how I want to spend my old age.

We're all her muthafuckahs, Trey. Men say they want to screw this woman or that woman, but what they really want to do is back the screw out, they want to unscrew the woman, undo her integrity, her intactness, her privacy. Women's privacy drives men mad. Some men. For others it's an endless delight, a kind of affirmation of an afterlife. She's too much of something for them, so they want to unmake her. They want to fuck something out of her, and it happens to be the humanity upon which civilization depends. What men want to do to women is exactly what they want to do to the world. What they do to the world is what they do to women in their heads. What I want, Trey, is that nobody should ever undo this girl, change her, mess with her. That's all I want. And I recognize that it's a much harder ambition than wanting to be rich. I should know. It's much more elusive. And, and—but I'll never tell you this—it can get a person in much more trouble. That's the song of your Woolf-tan Ertugay, Trey. Maybe his aubade.

***

Would the wind be so kind as to turn this page? I'm not ready for this from a man I have trouble liking. If somebody is going to say things like this you ought to like him. Or hate him. Any of it. What is familiar about this, like a story my paternal grandmother Katife told me? Trey doesn't approve of this girl he's using, this girl he knows so much about. To me she's Artemis, to Trey a criminal, a butcher, perhaps a murderer. I clench the wolf's head of my cane, the alternative being to crack Trey's skull with it. The man has earned my dislike. How much do we have to pay for what we want to know? This man is exacting an awful price. Must be genetic. But, really, is this the way to respond to a man who's just said something exquisite? I've never entertained such a creative idea about man's relationship to woman, have I? Much as he ought to be and seems to be, the man is not a poot.

Trey is thrilled by Wulftan's discomfort. The man will never know the truth, but this is enough to torment him. A lie is so much more aromatic than the metallic smell of truth. Power is suggesting you might impart something you're never going to impart, something you might not even have. Maybe that's the secret behind Grace's gesture in the lobby. I haven't really got anything for you, so I'll just shoot you, figuratively speaking, or not.

***

I'm a crank, Trey continues. That's why Boudica takes care of me. I met her here two years ago. I was sitting on a bench making faces at baby monsters being pushed around by Mommy Nazis—that's what I call those rich bitches who think they've got a right to mow you down with their strollers just because their husbands thieve in Brioni suits.

She was walking north on the path that parallels Fifth Avenue just before you get to The Metropolitan Museum. Girlie, girlie, I say, you're too young to talk to yourself. Who the fuck told you you could call me girlie? she says. It wasn't very respectful, I say. I'm used to the Stroller Nazis, I consider them only half human, I say, hoping to get on her good side. She knows right off who I mean. She stares at me for a few seconds and then flops down next to me. I'd taken the wind out of her sails, you might say.

So, what're you, a child molester?

What, I'm a what? I say.

Yeah, me too, she says. Ya wanna buy me a hotdog?

Will you think I want something for it?

Oh yeah, I look helpless, right? she says.

I'm playing who-will be-my-heir that day. Like I'm a stranger I'm observing. Aren't we all observing our stranger selves?

Each time we meet I doubt Trey's story a little more. I know he has encountered Grace. But whose story is this? Whose embroidery? What is going on here? We're helping him die, Grace, me, who else? One by one he gives his atoms away. Today they rhyme, everything, everyone. Tomorrow not. Rad, the shoeshine man, he should be a Rad. It doesn't matter, time is short, there's much to do, and in the end we're nameless, nameless as we ought to be. I no longer trust anything Trey Godling says, but this is our project now, and I'm not sure where Boudica/Grace fits in. Everyone needs a figment. This is Trey's dying figment. Will it be mine? What is the man talking about? Is this the final stage of his illness? Two years ago...? She's been taking care of him for two years? He must need killing. Giving his atoms away... I understand, but I don't. I couldn't impress a professor with this knowledge, but I know what Trey is doing. Two years, my ass! Boudica told this story to Jean-Luc. She told him about her encounter with me, and now this wicked old coot is playing it back to me, embellishing, pretending he met her in this park. But when she told it to Jean-Luc, not knowing, of course, Jean-Luc uses gossip to trade in the market, did she say she met me? Did she amend her story, did she say, Hey, Jean-Luc, you know the old fart I told you about in the park, well, he's the same old fart you work for at Number Two Sutton? Is that what happened? And now Trey Godling is conflating all this gossip, aggrandizing himself, tormenting me. Too bad Carl Jung is dead. I'd go see him and tell him about all this synchronicity. He'd make something out of it. What the hell am I going to make out of it?

We must be very careful how we give ourselves away, Trey says one day, just as if he heard me say it. Trey doesn't want to be me, but some days he sounds like it. I never wanted to be anyone else, not as beautiful as Alain Delon, not even as smart as Wittgenstein, but I've always had trouble watching flowers die, scents fade, certain presences leave. I don't want Boudica, but I don't want her to leave, anyone, anything. I want her to make the world fragrant. And this towering ambition I can't finance, I'm not rich enough, although I suspect I'm infinitely richer than Trey.

Yes! Trey leans forward into my face. Nothing, nothing stinks like people who want to keep on being themselves, Woolf-tan. Ask the undertakers. They smell worse than tobacco smoke in wet wool. They're fetid. They don't smell like people. They're not. That's what I learned from what she told me about Poe Torrance....

***

Trey should not be allowed to go further. He'll just babble. All he knows is secondhand, and Jean-Luc has told him only enough to bait him. Jean-Luc himself doesn't know much more. But Trey has given me an opening here, yammering about people who want to keep on being themselves. They certainly have bad taste. Poe Torrance just wanted to be himself, and men like that are always up to no good. We're answerable, and he refused to be. He was no fool. When he bought the cabin on the Arendskill flood plain the first thing he did was chop away the cement retainer that sealed off the crawl space. The former owner, a cement layer from Corona, thought it made the cabin look substantial, but Poe saw right away it was rotting out the sills and stringers. Poe was practical, but that's hardly enough to recommend anybody.

Grace was eight when he bought the cabin. Her mom ran off with a zonked-out jazz trumpeter who played nights on street corners and spent his days selling balloons and whining, *Make the kiddies happy.* She was nine when her home became an island. The Arendskill went on one of its rampages and cut them away from its north bank. Poe built a wooden bridge and started parking his truck in a hutch on the far side of the bridge.

He liked to say they lived at the epicenter of the Catskills. He read that in a state brochure. They hunted deer and fished for brown trout. He wasn't a bad guy until she sprouted tits. It was downhill after that. He kept staring at them and there wasn't much she could talk to him about. She spent a lot of time on a bike an old farmer scrapped together for her. That's how she got to the library, with her tits intruding on her life and feeling desperate about Poe's misplaced eyes.

Something was going to happen, and when she started spotting her pants she was sure of it. She had to do a lot of reading to figure out what to do. When Poe started climbing into bed with her she figured she was already behind the curve. Then the Arendskill solved everything. On April 15th, 2004, it spun the cabin around, tore out the bridge and sent it churning downstream, and carried away half their island.

Thumbing to New York City she thought she ought to talk like some of the books she read, like Louise Erdrich and that British lady, Barbara Pym, not like Poe and his dumb-shit buddies. How hard would that be? She liked the words. She liked looking them up. And she bet New York City had libraries that stayed open. And if men were going to stare at her tits, well, she could see they weren't going to get in anybody's way, and she liked her tits that way, unambitious as they were. She could tell they were never going to be boobs, so loose shirts were the ticket.

The man who might not have to be anything again has been thinking for six months about what he wishes he'd said when Grace Torrance plopped down on his park bench. It irks him that Trey seems to have said the right things in similar circumstances, but can he take Trey's word for it? No, it's all bullshit. But it's convincing. Trey seems to have guessed what Wulftan wishes he'd said. Okay, Dr. Jung, what's that about? He finds a way to express his suspicion the next time he meets Trey.

Here's what I think, Trey. Most people are like the moon, they reflect other people's expectations. But you absorb them. I think you're dying of having absorbed too much of other people's light.

At this moment every sound in Manhattan becomes distinct, discernible. Imagine a city without white noise. Imagine knowing every sound and where it comes from. Trey doesn't think he can survive Wulftan's words. Wulftan doesn't think he can survive having said them. He can't imagine a more terrible revenge for Trey's toying with him. His pity for the man aches in his stomach.

Let's let this man talk directly to us for a while. But be warned, he's not as chatty as Trey Godling.

* * *

My name is Wulftan, meaning wolf power. I want you to know that. I want you to know about my mother Friede. My father Alp not so much. He was a sanitation engineer, a.k.a. garbage man in Cologne. You don't need to know about him. But you would have liked Friede. Now it's too late. I'll never see her again. That's what happens when your brain sinks to your shoes, squish, squish.

All right, thank you, thank you very much, Wulftan, and now a few words from our sponsors.

Many sonsofbitches need killing. If not, I wouldn't be rich. But I never before cared which sonofabitch needed killing.

Life is like a quilt, his mother used to say. It's not enough to know what piece to use next, you have to see it coming together in your head. She showed him pictures of rolling farmland, each patch a different shape and color. It made him dizzy. He felt like a bird or someone in a Chagall painting, flying. Friede laughed when he told her this. Yes, she cried, my dizzy bird!

Something's coming together. It's in the air. Encountering Grace Torrents in the park, the sonofabitch who needed killing, Beryl Payne's strange remark, Trey Godling's tall story, Grace shooting him in the lobby with her finger. A big crazy quilt making him dizzy. Many patches to fly over, enough to make any bird dizzy. He never liked quilts for this reason. He always imagined himself a bird flying over them and getting dizzy.

He walks to the little park at 57th and the river and looks downstream to U Thant Island, a ratty pile of riprap. I've come all this way from Germany, picking through carnage and treachery, to this genteel place and one of Friede's quilts. If you poured my ashes into the Narrows where would they go, the Elbe or the Bosporus? I don't know if we're our genes. An artist is more than his palette and brushes.

I've dealt with fanatics, crooks, madmen, dictators, Swiss bankers, Wall Street swindlers. I call Donald Trump Donald and the mayors David, Ed and Mike, forget that schmuck, what's-his-name, Rudy. But now it's Luis the doorman, Patrick the manager, an angry teenager, a dying swell, a morphing socialite… the chosen ones, the ones Wulftan Ertugay chooses for his own unaccountable reasons. I don't have to explain a thing and neither do they, not even Ms. Grace Torrents. We don't really have to, do we, explain ourselves, that is? The river is full of wrecks, Dutchmen, Frenchmen, Spanish, bones and their dinner plates in suck-holes now, and it's rearranging its furniture and not explaining a damned thing. Wrecks in Trey Godling's backyard. And what I'm doing for him is not asking him to explain. Now that's better than blowing up an airplane or something Wagnerian like that.

Those vortices in that black water there, the wrecks of dreams, ambitions, shifting like restless people in bed, are trying to find the right position, roiling the surface on this haunted river. This is the cemetery of nations. Trey is a caretaker of sorts, with his townhouse backing on the estuary of our cares.

**

What is Jean-Luc Plamandon willing to do to get what he wants? Wasn't that Beryl Sutphen's question? Trey Godling is what Jean-Luc Plamandon is willing to do. They met at Cooper Union when Jean-Luc was studying there. Trey didn't act rich, he didn't dress rich, but he sounded rich, and Jean-Luc sniffs wealth better than any Madison Avenue clerk. Trey was one of Jean-Luc's few teachers who didn't yak. He just showed Jean-Luc how to paint. Hans Hofmann was gone, so Jean-Luc settled for Trey.

You're very observant, he said to Jean-Luc once as they headed out for coffee in Astor Place. I mean, you notice that I paint with both hands, but you never say anything.

It's your business.

That's not precisely so, because it makes it difficult for you learn from me, don't you think?

I think life is about the one hand not knowing what the other is doing.

Yes, but two left hands is an extraordinary handicap.

Two left hands? Why not two right hands?

No, both my hands obey the same impulse. I'm doubly left-handed. It has dire consequences, and I love them all. I have a more intelligent brushstroke than Dali. There's more emotional intelligence in it.

If it was meant to get a rise out of his student, it didn't. Jean-Luc simply nodded. Claiming to be the nation's savior isn't even in the same league with claiming to have a better brushstroke than Dali. You should be as reckless as Caravaggio to make such a claim.

With Trey's backing he conceived and started Morton Street Art Preparators. Trey gave so much money to museums and sat on so many boards that he was prepared to appreciate Jean-Luc's idea, approve it and send him clients. And all Jean-Luc had to do was indulge Trey's occasional but pervy sexual passions. Both men happened to like each other a bit more than they liked the women in their lives. But neither could imagine a life without women.

And then came the ambush, just as casually as Jean-Luc had followed Grace and The Queen in Union Square Park....

This girl and her giantess, Jean-Luc, you put them up in your storage space?

Caretakers. It works out well. They work for me, they mind the paintings, and I just clear out a little samizdat space for a kitchenette and bath. I'm teaching them to help me move and install. The girl has a better brushstroke than you, Trey. Hofmann would have eaten her colors.

You think this will hurt me, don't you?

Hurt's not my style, you know that. It's just the truth.

Why do you admire this little redneck doxy?

Didn't I just give enough reason to admire anybody? Boo isn't a doxy. She isn't little. She isn't a redneck. And the only reason you're asking is because you've been watching her and you've developed a rash. She's lissome and struck clean through with madness, like a rare ballerina. She remembers the rattle in her crib and every look anyone ever gave her, and some people know it to look at her. She even remembers the things you didn't say.

Would you sell her to me? Would you sell Boudica to me?

What're you offering? (Jigging the fly in front of the trout is common in the art world.)

I'll think of some way to make it rewarding to you both. Would you trust me to do that? You've told me every kind of story about her. I feel I know her. I want to know her. I want her to tell the stories of her days to me. After all, she remembers them all, doesn't she? Do you know how rare that is? I want to buy a little Scheherazade. Everybody will profit.

She comes with The Queen.

That's interesting. What have you gleaned about their relationship? That's a mountain of flesh, Jean-Luc. Do you three play together?

***

This light isn't going to change. It's stuck. Forget amber, forget green. Chuck your life in the gutter and never turn back. Sometimes that's the one good thing you can do with your life and if you don't you're fucked even though you call it expedience. This light is never going to change. You go down into the subway to depart a world that is never going to change. That's why subways haunt our imaginations. We hope, we pray they take us to near dimensions, dimensions we sense but can't prove.

Nothing will rub Trey's words out of the air. Nor Wulftan's revenge. Call it any damned thing you choose and it will still be ink hanging in the air, ready to splash you if you try to get around it. There is no passing by. Worse, there are your words hanging in the air, and your face is always going to be blackened by them. Each man has hung an ink splotch in the air in front of the other.

Jean-Luc wishes the subway would never stop, would submarine into the Atlantic because now there's nowhere to go home to. His glue is unstuck. He shouldn't have smiled as Trey spoke. His face should have reflected his horror. Puke burns high in his throat. He should have puked on Trey. And before that he should never have told the old fuck anything about Grace, because he hadn't liked the way Trey had wet his lips. As happens so often, he'd seen it coming and pretended he hadn't. He'd stood in front of the train and done nothing, and now he was a facsimile of Jean-Luc. Each time this sort of thing happens the ink fades a little more, and after a while you're a blank piece of paper with a few traces of what you had been or could have been.

Jean-Luc is determined to do this. It doesn't matter what the girl wants. She owes him. And if she doesn't know how to do it, he'll teach her like he's taught her everything else. She's going to do it, because their lives depend on it.

Singleness of purpose, getting what you want depends on not letting your mind spin. Shake Grace the person out of your mind. Let only the idea of her in. Trey isn't buying the girl. He's buying the idea. It will have a fancy name. We're a nation of packagers. But everything will be swept away in Styrofoam barges. He thought of a waiter whipping a tablecloth out from under china and flatware. It was an haute cuisine restaurant, now it's a beery bistro. Everything is the same, but everything is different.

***

Trey reasons another way. I'm dead when I don't want a few things enough to dream about their scents. Everything's olfactory. That's what Joyce is all about, an author of fragrances. You have to nose your way through *Ulysses*. If paint were odorless I'd sculpt or engineer massacres like Wulftan-What's-His-Name who never wears a hat. The girl has something in her I want to hold in my hand. I think it's her dignity, her natural dignity. I'll give it back to her. But of course it will be soiled. Everything must be soiled. Nothing is as profane as bed sheets. Everything is viral. Everything has a handle and nothing is as filthy as that handle. I have a few contagions for her. The giantess I don't know about. She comes with that zingy Catskill thyme. I'll improvise. I think I'd like to paint the giant with sable brushes. Not a canvas, but her. Blue like a Pict, some crimson streaks—wounds—we'll see. She'll enjoy it. Then what, I don't know. I don't really want to fuck anybody. I never have. It's seamy business. But I have this passion for getting in the wood, the bone, the steel, the secrets, into beads of sweat, tears, effusions. I dream of taking tea in a tear. I know I'm particular about whose tear it is, but I never remember in the morning, never, even though I lie in wait for the name with a bedside glass of water half full and a pen and pad nearby. Heaven would be knowing the tear's name, but I have no illusions.

Jean-Luc wants to know about all this, but he can't have it. He's going to have to come up with the girl on my terms. I didn't mean to make him pay for my help, but now I do. It's what I need to die. Artists know what they need, the rest is shit. Jean-Luc is going to produce. He's had it a bit too easy. There are consequences to whetting someone's appetite. This isn't his comeuppance, it's his coming of age. He'll look back on me the way vampires look on their makers. One must soil fortunate lads to understand the nature of death. I did say that, didn't I? What shit! And yet I feel the truth in it behind my navel. This is how I want to die, making that boy cough up. The girl is incidental, but I know she's going to taste good, like a caviar cafeteria.

***

We're all waiting for the killer of the sonofabitch, all heightening the suspense by denying we know the sonofabitch. And there's no better place to wait than on a bench facing east in Central Park. The sun has a special incestuous way of entering Manhattan. It doesn't want to wake it up. It wants to stand in the shadow of a doorway and observe its populous nakedness. The sun tickles Wulftan Ertugay's toes, Montauk and the North Fork. Then it warms his knees, Babylon, then it commits a little arson in his stomach, Corona, and finally it burns through the East Side high-rises to melt his cataracts. Queens is the sun's pee, Hoboken its evening piss. Meanwhile it dribbles bright red down Manhattan's legs.

The United States is my ass end, my fat in the fire. I am facing Mecca. I have made a great deal of trouble for its European impediment, brushing it aside with my left hand, making my ablutions in the Mediterranean, leaning with my right hand on North Africa, touching my head to the Kaaba. I will fart America away and propel myself to Asia. I will… Gabriel is opening his arms. Welcome, welcome, Wulftan. You've made a lot of trouble in the world, you high-nosed wolf, but all is forgiven. Recite the kalima and come home. What bullshit! There's only one thing I like about my father's faith: everything belongs to God, everything we own is held in trust. That's all I like. Everything I own is held in trust. I'm just kidding, Gabriel, I'm not ready yet. Not yet. Friede means elf strength. Believing that, you can't respect a brick-and-mortar religion. Alp never gave a shit about her name. I never forgot its meaning, and I don't now.

***

Pat, how many people can get into my apartment?

Well, there's me, the two handymen, the door captain. Tell ya the truth, Mr. Ertugay, there's more'n there ought to be. But it's the way the board set it up. I try to keep an eye on it. Oh yeah, there's Catarina, your housekeeper. I was kinda surprised to see the cops. Did they find anything?

No, no sign of break-in, that's why I asked you, Pat. Not a scratch, nothing.

So what's missing, Mr. Ertugay, if ya don't mind my askin'?

Let me show you something, Patrick. Here, see this, isn't it incredible?

You don't manage a building like No. 2 without seeing a lot of fine art. It rubs off on you. Hell, Pat has hung a lot of it, although people like Beryl Sutphen and Wulftan Ertugay would never let anybody but an art preparator hang a painting. Mr. Ertugay had a preference for abstract geometric artists like Josef Albers, Kazimir Malevich, Piet Mondrian, I. Rice Pereira, but this painting was maybe 12 or 13 inches wide and eight inches high.

That's it, Patrick, nothing's missing, something has been added. Go on, take it over to the window, Patrick. Take your time. Tell me what you think.

Pat Noonan had looked into some women's eyes like this, he'd stared into the barrel of guns like this. It was like opening your little bathroom window in the city and seeing a falcon land on the sill and stare at you. It was like that one face in a crowd that makes you rub your sobbing chest. The colors were like liquefied jewels: rubies, emeralds, sapphires, opals. The paint was laid on like the rolling, dizzying hills of Delaware County—they invited him to become a nanobot and travel them. The little painting made him dizzy. He thought of driving off between the brushstrokes in a Maserati. The little painting filled him with yearning and hurt his chest. Wulftan Ertugay was the only person in America who thought Pat Noonan capable of such sentiments.

Whuddya call it, Mr. Ertugay, it's so small?

A miniature, Patrick. It takes incredible skill. And do you know where I found it?

He's gonna say he bought it in Tompkins Square for five bucks, right? He rescued it from the trash room.

I found it in the pajama drawer in my bedroom, right next to my plastic Glock, you know, the one that slips through airport detectors.

A plastic Glock, Mr. Ertugay?

Wulftan looked as if Patrick was pulling his leg. Patrick knew as much about small weaponry as Wulftan did, maybe more.

Yes, I know you know about such things, Patrick. You know Glocks from Brownings and 47s from Uzis. But what was it doing there?

Ya never saw it before?

That's part of my dismay, Patrick. But what's important here is the painting. Look at it. What do you think it's doing?

Doin'? Do paintings do something?

Patrick had made a career out of professing ignorance.

Oh yes, my dear Patrick, that's their purpose, their real purpose. Paintings do you. A gun just has to look like a tattooed thug until it does the one thing it was meant to do. But a painting is changing things moment by moment, even when nobody is looking at it. Why do you think I collect paintings? If what I'm saying isn't true I'd collect coins or stamps. You think paintings just break up walls like pictures in a newspaper? You think they're tombstones? Doors, windows maybe. No, my friend, they change your chemistry, they fiddle with your vital signs, they monitor them, they perform surgery on you. Nano-surgery is child's play compared to what paintings do. They're very dangerous, why do you suppose I'm so choosy? Do you think I would let Winton Payne's exorbitant junk in my apartment? No wonder the man gets more stupid by the day. You think this building's value is in real estate? This building is an alembic, Patrick. Its elements are changing things. The merchant banks think they're in charge, but the museums, Patrick, and the private collections and the artists' studios are in charge. Without them the world is junk, worthless junk.

Patrick's tired face recovers some of its youthful beauty. This is what I came here for, not to get away from Tommy or MI-6 or the goddam boys, but for this, to hear this. He remembers a hill of daisies. I came here to know this old man, to hear what he makes of this terrible place, this world where people kill each other for a handful of superstitions. I'm where I ought to be. How do ya like that? Never was in Ireland, but here I am, at home.

Wulftan knows Patrick thinks ill of Payne and Trey Godling, just the kind of swells who'd abused the Irish for generations. And everybody else, too. Trey had enlisted Patrick to find a work crew to renovate an upstairs room and had kept him waiting six months for payment. Patrick rarely let his face convey his thoughts. That's part of what you get paid for running a building like Number Two. But he let Wulftan read his face because they had seen much of the same thing.

Wulftan—it's unmistakably him—sits like an Ottoman khedive in a field of tulips, wearing the kind of turban that the tulips suggested, and scattered all around him, like Omar Khayyam's guest stars on the grass, are little children wearing bright turbans, and off in the distance is a grand Ottoman ship with its distinctive rig of burgundy square and lateen sails. An eclipsed moon is hung in the sky. Nightingales are dispersed in the sea of tulips. The painting is worthy of a caliph's gift to a czar.

It's the strangest thing Pat has ever seen, but in Wulftan it stirs memories he can't possibly have. The rapt expressions of the children, the humor in the khedive's face enthrall him. He seems to be shaping an invisible orb for the children. They see it, but after all these years he cannot. He is making something for them. The children's hands are raised in wonder, their palms turned towards him. He loves these children. Where is the world in which this is happening, happening now? How can he get there? His own hands rise to the level of his belt. Wulftan notices and an idea forms in mind and lights his amber eyes. He brushes back his satiny gray hair.

Ya know Ms. Beryl, right, Mr. Ertugay? Well, she has this teacher does something called bio-energy. They make basketballs of energy with their hands, and their hands get hot, and they toss these balls of energy around. And you can see about two inches of gray stuff, they call it ether, around their fingers. I've seen it. Their faces change. They glow.

Patrick, you are so observant.

Yeah, that's why I'm still alive.

I think you know just what you're talking about, just what you're seeing, Patrick. But who do you think put this little masterpiece next to my plastic Glock? Who do you think sandwiched it in my pajamas? I'm telling you, Patrick, the fact that someone put it in that exact spot interests me even more than how that someone got into the place.

Well, here's a thought, Mr. E, this person likes you. I mean, it coulda been a bomb.

Mmm, yes, a bomb, Patrick. Mr. E winked. What kind of bomb would you think?

I wouldn't know, Mr. E.

Yes, you would, Patrick. And if you had put it there they'd be rebuilding the top of this building.

This burglar, Mr. E, whoever it is, broke in to give you

something. What is that, reverse B&E? What would the cops charge this guy with? Criminal generosity, ya think?

Oh God, that's funny, Patrick. I know a man, you do too, who would like that phrase.

Practically every suit in this building would like it.

Would W. X. Payne?

That prick.

Now about this liking me, Patrick. As in liking something about me, maybe things I don't know? Does anybody in this building paint, Patrick?

The super's face screws up comically. Ya puttin' me on, Mr. E? Nobody's that criminal-generous here.

I like putting you on, Patrick. I know you know a lot about interrogations. I think you probably entertained the Brits when they weren't slapping you around.

Yeah, sounds like you, Mr. E, when you think about it. I mean, you and me have these conversations and we like each other because you know things about me I don't know.

Mmm, and you know things about me you'd never admit, Patrick. We've seen a lot of shit, you and I, and we know things are never under any circumstances what they seem to be. That's quite fortunate, don't you think?

If I didn't know that I'd be working for the MTA.

Or rotting in a Tommy prison.

Or a Belfast dump.

Wait here for a minute, Patrick. We have something to celebrate. I don't know what, exactly, but I'm sure we do.

In a few minutes Wulftan reappears carrying a silver tray with a bottle and two glasses.

Macallan 1926, Patrick. We shall drink to this unknown artist, this unsigned masterpiece, to our friendship. I think we've got each other's backs, as they say. Here's to... to all the deadly business in the world that passes for nothing, nothing at all.

That's a damn-strange toast...

Wulftan, Patrick, call me Wulftan when we're alone. Otherwise I'm condescending when I call you Patrick, don't you think? And I have a feeling nobody called you Pat back when it was best if nobody called you anything at all. Am I right about that?

A damn-strange toast, Mr. E, only I just happen to know what you mean. It's the usual bullshit that kills us, not us stupid bombers. And no, nobody ever called me Pat, but Tommy, he called me Mr. Noonan like it rhymed with something. Yes, many things ought to rhyme with Noonan, but do they? Now Ertugay, every damned little thing rhymes with Ertugay.

Mmm, to the usual bullshit then, of which we see bountiful plenty in this very building. And, you know, if I never discover the secret operative who made this painting, who rifled my apartment, who put it next to my plastic Glock, I don't think I really give a damn. I have a friend in this building and I have a friend out there who thinks I'm a goddamn tulip, and what more lovely thing would I be, Patrick?

To the Lovely Tulip then, Wulftan. Yer a lovely tulip.

And to the wisest bomber.

Patrick Noonan was out the door and headed for the chained-in-place freight elevator when he turned and walked back to Wulftan, who was still standing in the hallway. You belong in that field, you do. That's why you go to the park. You don't go to feed the pigeons or watch the young ones. You grow there.

There's something our magic artist missed, Patrick. You know the Christmas rose? Some people call it the lenten rose. It's the first flower to bloom in spring, even when there's still snow on the ground. Its real name is hellebore and it's a deadly poison. I'm a hellebore. I fantasize about giving a brunch and serving hellebore hors d'oeuvres. Hellebore is ground cover. I cover a lot of ground, don't you think, Patrick?

You think I don't know how beautiful the lenten rose is, doncha, Wulftan? But this artist's no fool. It's safe to be a tulip. Everybody likes a tulip. A tulip's a cup. What's in the cup?

Wulftan turns and goes inside his apartment. Must I be a tulip? Can't I wear a snow coat, look lovely and innocent, and be as deadly as hell? Isn't that me? Must all old men play it safe and look like a tulip? Patrick has made me very sad. Why doesn't this burglar-artist see the hellebore in me? I don't want to tiptoe through the tulips. I don't want to sit among them either. But I know that khedive is me. I know those children love me. I know we ooh and ah together as we share knowledge no adult can possess. That's what the khedive and the children are doing, sharing knowledge. Who could possibly know this about me, who could imagine it? Who could have thought this much about me? And why? All I want to do with the rest of my life is raise my hands palms out—and the children will appear and worlds will pass between us. Who could know this for me?

Pour yourself another of the Macallan, Wulftan.

Patrick returns and knocks on the door.

Ya didn't tell the cops about the painting, didja now? Okay, well, see, now yer what they call a co-conspirator. I mean, somebody breaks in, doesn't take a thing, and leaves you a gift, and you're worried about the break-in and what the gift means, right? It's not a security matter. Ya don't wanna be like Homeland Security. This ain't a red or yellow alert, Wulftan.

So what is it, Patrick?

One night in Londonderry I got a snootful. I started singing. I have this counter tenor, ya know. It's kinda rare. Catches the attention of the priests, unfortunately. There's this guy staring at me from across the pub. Do I know Mick from Limey? Not always. Sometimes. This guy could be either, like me. I leave after a while and I start walking. This guy comes outta an alley and throws me up against the wall. He's a fuckin' British Army intelligence officer. I know you, Patrick Noonan, he sez. Then he lets go of me and says, Nice tenor. And that's it. He's gone. So what is it, Wulftan? Who the fuck knows? But I wasn't lookin' fer no trouble, and neither was Tommy, not that night, maybe because I sang my heart out. Didja sing yer heart out for anybody lately, Wulftan, I hafta ask ya?

***

It's getting to the point, Jean-Luc, where I don't care. The food is spoiling. I'm spoiling. The girl is getting long in the tooth.

Six months, Jean-Luc, more than enough time to persuade the girl of her best interests. It's not as if I'm going to hang around long enough to gloat. I've told her entire life story to some old goat in the park while you've dragged your feet. Why would you try me when your entire lifestyle depends on this? You haven't grown a conscience in the wrong place, have you?

Your looks and your charm won't get you out of this, you know. I'll take you down if you make a fool out of me. You know that, don't you? You don't think I paint so well because I'm timid, do you? You're weak, Jean-Luc, that's why you're a mediocre painter. You don't have the stomach for the improbable stroke, so you noodle around it. That's what makes second-rate painters. They pussyfoot around the moment they choose not to confront. Their work needs ornate frames and lots of critical disquisition. The bad painters need the big-mouthed critics.

Here's the situation. You produce the girl or you kill me. Which do you have the stomach for? I'm ready to pull the rug out from under you. Your calls and e-mails won't be answered. Everyone you know will be busy. In a month you won't be able to pay your rent, and the Jean-Luc Plamandon empire will be swept up by syphilitic John Does in blue coveralls. You'll be carted off in blue barrels, Jean-Luc. I'm the moment you've been waiting for. You had better rise to my occasion. Who knows, you might even learn how to paint. There is an expendable girl behind every great work of art, bet on it. But you're a charmer, not a bettor. Girls are always in training to be expendable, Jean-Luc. They're currency.

***

Jean-Luc missteps like dance innovations, and not just with his feet. What he presents as a caprice to Boo takes three months to set in as a reality, and when it does he starts eyeing scissors warily. She never says a word when he says, when he finally has to say, I'm serious, Boo. I owe this guy everything, and it's such a little thing. He's dying. He probably won't even touch you. He just wants... but he couldn't say what, didn't know what, and it didn't matter. Poe Torrance never did anything this

152

bad, and he can't charm it to look like anything but what it is. Boo knows all about the "just wants" of the world, and they're neither fair nor almost.

Jean-Luc doesn't think Boo told The Queen. If she had, well, there's another unknown. Defenestration comes to mind. Boo wouldn't tell The Queen. Or anybody. Anybody but him. He's the repository of her story. He knows about Eunuch Poe. She trusts him, had trusted him. And it's probably her story that appeals to Trey more than she does. And Boo doesn't really know, not firsthand, what happens when you appeal to a man, what happens afterwards. She knows nobody thinks that about her. But as far as she's concerned she's a virgin because Poe doesn't count. He can't count, because if he did count, then there would be nothing to look forward to, and now Jean-Luc, who did count, is trying to give her nothing to look forward to all over again. It's one thing to remember every day of your life, it's another thing to worry about the next day. The only reason she's here, the only reason she can draw and paint is because when the moment comes Boo lives in it, she doesn't ask it to wait, she doesn't slide around it, and she doesn't negotiate with it.

And what would Boo tell The Queen, that she's thinking about it? That she's confused? The Queen is one of those people who get along in the world just so long as that certain button isn't touched, and her buttons are well concealed. She can tell you how high a building is, she can keep up with a cash register, she can walk into a school and solve the problems on a blackboard, but that's all she'll let you know. Nobody important in her life detects a Down East accent, but they know it isn't from Da Bronx.

You're so vivid you vibrate, Grace. That's what Lois Witte told her. And you want your colors to vibrate, Grace. You want to draw and paint with such certainty that the current is always on. You want your work to be always on. Boo thought she understood Lois, but when she started going to museums and galleries she saw that some artists shake the air around them and they create images that shake the air. You can get downright seasick staring at

153

some paintings. Titian comes to mind. You not only can drown in his waves, you want to drown in them. Or you can poke around the particles we're made of in a Seurat. Boo likes to think about rearranging *A Sunday Afternoon on the Island of the Grand Jatte*. She has painted it a hundred ways in her head.

Boo remembers what Lois said every day. Each miniature is testament to Lois's words. Do you like this, Lois? Sometimes Lois says no and Boo starts all over again. This means the track of every sable hair on the canvas counts. Nobody knows, nobody can imagine what a perfectionist Boo is. Jean-Luc suspects, but she's never let him see her real work, her finished work. He just knows she can draw better than anyone at Cooper Union and handles paint as if she'd made it. His heart races when he sees Boo draw or paint. She should be studying at Cooper Union, not him. They would give her scholarships just to see her draw with such purity.

He knows—and here's the real betrayal—that Boo isn't the sum of her parts, she isn't her story, she's a work in progress, and he no more knows what that girl will do than Eunuch Poe did. But he's beginning to wonder if Trey thinks he knows. Is that man looking for the girl to kill him? Better she should kill me, Jean-Luc thinks. Yes, this is your moment, Jean-Luc. You can no more deal with Boo than anyone could deal with Caravaggio. But he is Boo's only patron, while the Lombard engineer of light had many.

***

The more Boo thinks of Jean-Luc and the other fuck, the more she thinks about Beryl and Mister Wolf's-Head Cane. Some people spend a lot of time rewiring their brains. Boo thinks of her brain as a bog along the Arendskill; you never know where a marsh light is going to appear. If Beryl and Wulftan wink like swamp gas in her thoughts there must be a reason, and the reason must be related to whatever is bothering her. Why is it she seems to be the only one who takes Beryl seriously? Is she the only one? Who wouldn't take Beryl seriously? Same person who might not take Boo seriously, right? You can skate around the city being canny and cunning, which isn't quite like having ordinary savvy or street smarts. Or you can be yourself and see what happens, which is all Boo knows how to be, because everything else she's tried itches. So, being herself, she instinctively knew Wulftan Ertugay wasn't out to jump her bones. And she knew Beryl regarded her as some sort of faerie she'd found under a mushroom. None of which helped her respond to Jean-Luc's proposition. Well, it was a command, really. Or was it? Now you wouldn't rely on swamp lights to guide you through a bog, would you? Unless of course you're a faerie.

If Jean-Luc knew how Boo was thinking he'd be even more clueless than he is at the moment.

Wulftan Ertugay doesn't put a gloss on anything, but it bothers her she didn't sense this right away. That's why she shot him in the lobby with her finger, because it bothered her she'd dissed him, and now it bothers her she shot him. The other fuck doesn't matter. He doesn't deserve a response, not from her. The more she thinks of Jean-Luc and the other fuck, the more she thinks about Beryl and Wulftan. Jean-Luc doesn't know about her climbing fire escapes and breaking into apartments, he doesn't know about the miniatures. He just knows her natural, left-handed talent far exceeds his own, and like a damned fool he's happy about it, and his being happy to find talent in her is what seals their friendship. Is that what you'd call it? Their relationship? No, you wouldn't call it a friendship or a relationship. It's a deal. A big deal. A name would spoil it. And now it's so spoiled everything tastes bad, even fresh cannolis. Even knowing he takes pleasure in her skill has gone bad. He doesn't know why the corners of her mouth turn up and down, he doesn't know it's because she remembers everything. He thinks she has a snapshot memory, that she thinks like a PowerPoint show. He doesn't suspect that everything she sees is a piece of a puzzle, and her mouth turns up and down according to which part of it she's solved, and how it tastes to have solved it.

***

Trey is telling her second-hand story, her hand-me-down story to Wulftan, the real crux of her deliberations. And while Trey twists facts and plays time like an accordion Jean-Luc hears every clock, every watch in the city ticking. There's only so long you can do this, then your ears bleed. He knows that he, Beryl Sutphen, Wulftan Ertugay, Patrick Noonan, Trey Godling, The Queen are all parts of the same clock. Only Boo stands outside. His grand idea comes to him like a second hand faltering before midnight. The silence pushes out the windows. Sometimes in a great crisis it's better to do nothing at all, and Jean-Luc decides to celebrate doing nothing at all. Celebrate it big, handsomely, dangerously. The more he thinks of it the more he likes it. It's the kind of impulse that brought him to Trey, to Boo, and if they never see each other again, if one of them perishes in this predicament, the other will always revere this beau geste. Grace returns. He smiles at the pun on Boo's given name. Yes, he's a pimp, but his habitual grace hasn't forsaken him, not yet. His beau geste will be like a Viking funeral. It's unknown at this moment who the corpse will be. It doesn't matter. The dragon ship, the fire, and the people standing on the beach matter.

***

Maybe it comes from growing up among long shadows and rushing water, but Boo has always believed that she feels people thinking about her. Once on a school trip to an old factory building in Kingston where a lot of artists had studios she happened on an aikido class. An instructor told her aikido is the art of using an attacker's energy, his momentum, to thwart him. She would have loved to join that class, but she did the next best thing, she went to the library in Phoenicia and read about aikido, and from that time on she's practiced a kind of remote aikido. When she senses someone thinking about her, if it doesn't feel good, she finds ways to feint and turn the attack back. But this idea is like Wulftan's plastic Glock or Beryl's underwear, nobody's business.

And all the while Trey is embellishing her second-hand story to Wulftan, the real crux of her deliberations. And that's why she feels he's already sold her and is just taking his time deciding how to package the goods.

A jazz thread, Blind Hoxie's music, binds these people. If they never see each other again, if one of them burns up in this fix, the others will revere this beau geste and always remember that once they lived, took a great chance, and got drunk on risk. Jean-Luc proposes a terrible thing, pours it into an alembic, administers the elixir of chance and possibility, adds a tincture of cruelty. The more Boo thinks about it the more her rage becomes something else. The muthafuckah has become something else. Yes, she shot the wrong person, and yes, Wulftan would have rather her finger had been a Glock, but the bullet went clear through him and embedded itself in a near future, in a beau geste. Like any good assassin, she policed her brass, she cleaned up her act by letting Jean-Luc know that she knows how vulgar it is to arrange the outcome of a truly dangerous thing. Cheap, like insider trading.

Wulftan too is thinking of a grand gesture. As in P.C. Wren's novel, he's thinking of Viking funerals. His bed is a fiery Viking ship sailing out to sea with his corpse, or a Sioux pallet burning on stilts on a fiery evening plain. Trey Godling wishes to leave with the girl, Wulftan Ertugay wishes to leave with dignity, and to that end he retools his will like a poem. And Patrick Noonan is the latest revision. I will give Patrick this marvelous little painting. He loves it. But I must decide how, when. I will leave Patrick some money, that's done, but this painting? I wish he had one of his own. That's what he needs. How can I arrange that? How will the burglar paint Patrick? He undoubtedly knows him. I must somehow commission a painting for Patrick from an artist I don't know or don't know I know.

***

Jean-Luc, I don't recall our having an appointment. There is only one thing I wish to discuss with you.

I didn't want you to prepare for this, Trey. I have this grand idea, a passion really. An unforgettable party, here, the whole ground floor and your garden out back on the river. I'd like to install something about the Dutch, French and British ships at the bottom of the river, a mural maybe. Everyone we know, all Morton Street's clients, your professional colleagues, your bankers, your favorite students—everyone who means something to you, Trey.

Hmm, I'm not sure you're one of them, Jean-Luc.

Trey, you asked a big thing, otherwise you wouldn't have had to threaten me.

I shouldn't have had to threaten you.

Whatever, but please listen. This will be a celebration of your life and at the heart of this celebration will be your finest acquisition, Boo...

I prefer Boudica.

No one should ever know what a person is really celebrating, Trey, you told me that yourself. It's straight out of your playbook. Remember you told me about your annual brunch for people you detest? Only the barman knows the truth. He has to know because he snockers the people you've targeted. Remember? He has to be someone famous, someone everyone wants to say they know. You even give him the privilege of snockering anybody whose face he doesn't like.

Me perhaps? Yes, yes, yes, Trey says, I do remember telling you, and I remember thinking of all the people I've shared this naughty little fact with who have sniggered and I remember thinking, This lovely boy, that would be you, Jean-Luc, doesn't have the face to snigger. He can't snigger. His face is too fine. Anyone whose face can snigger is not to be trusted, Jean-Luc. I'm sure that dreadful Chechen you cater to, what's his name, sniggers all the time. There is a certain sleazy mobility to faces that snigger, perhaps it's a Mediterranean thing.

Jean-Luc knows he means Wulftan Ertugay, a man he likes a good bit more than the Godling here, but his usefully chiseled face holds its secret. He is familiar with the dirty WASP habit of attributing the wrong ethnicity to people, coming as it does from a sense of having the only right ethnicity.

A party, you say? You would make the arrangements?

As I often have, Trey, of course. It must be formal. The people to whom you wish to say goodbye must be there, but of course there will be no goodbyes. That's too crass. A man should just disappear. I know you agree. The lighting will be special, Trey, a work of art itself.

And the girl, Boudica?

She can be a hostess. Everyone will get to see the focus of the celebration without knowing it. You never want guests to know what's really going on, do you? Parties are like Wall Street fleecings, the fewer in on the game the better. Everyone is invited to the game, but nobody knows its name.

It's all very clever, Jean-Luc, I admit, but I don't like you being in on the game. I don't trust you. You're the crazy-eyed Border collie bringing in the sheep.

That's the beauty of it, Trey. You don't have to trust me. It doesn't matter. I'm not going to be the barman. He must be lethally beautiful, like the young Joe Dallesandro or Vittorio Gassman.

Hmm, what about a woman? Yes, I might have several in mind. The kind you'd like to be beaten by.

Jean-Luc went directly to one of Trey's prized photo books and started leafing through one of them as if looking for just such a woman.

So what is it exactly that you purchase with this?

Your continued patronage, or at least your not withdrawing it.

I didn't offer you anything for the girl, you remember that, don't you? I merely told you what would happen if you didn't deliver.

And I always have delivered, Trey.

Mm, would you like a drink?

I think you should break out your Shipwrecked 1907 Heidsieck, Trey. This project is worthy of it. It's evening now. We can sit and watch the tugs and think of jolly Dutch widows who married shipwrecked Arab sailors before the British toned the town down.

Trey smiles, remembering how much he likes Jean-Luc's

outré whimsies. To jolly Dutch widows and wiry Arab sailors, to New Amsterdam, Jean-Luc! Reinhard, the 1907 Heidsieck, please, we're having a little fete here. The Calleija glasses, please. He winks at Jean-Luc because Jean-Luc is familiar with the diamond-studded champagne glasses cut from eight-kilo blocks of crystal.

***

I've never been the life of a party, them being the death of me.

People or the party? Patrick asks.

There's a difference? People aren't themselves at parties, says Wulftan, or they're too much of themselves. Either way, I hate them. Parties are like Cannes, they stink of exhibitionism. People are not themselves, or they are, and in either case I detest them. Parties bring out the quisling in people.

You fear them? People are unmasked, they're what you feared they've always been? Parties are where you find out you've been right all along, people are shits. But somehow you don't go home feeling righteous, do ya?

Dangerous shits, yes. I'd rather fight ethnic cleansers house to house.

Which ones? Serbs?

It doesn't matter, ethnic cleansers, partygoers, all deadly shits.

You don't think it's the drink?

Patrick Noonan hardly ever says anything to Wulftan Ertugay that doesn't interest Wulftan. A kind of opera dialogue goes on between them, part song, part metrical speech.

It's always going to be something. All parties should feature hellebore hors d'oeuvres, Patrick.

Patrick draws a blank.

Oh, it's believed hellebore, the lovely lenten rose, was used to poison Alexander the Great. Actually, I'd like to take a flame thrower to parties. They're like churches, Patrick, they exist to discomfit some and con everyone else.

Patrick grins. He knows a lot about this. Yer a lovely old devil, Wulftan.

***

Lovely old devil and sadly handsome bomber will, of course, be at Trey's swish shebang, Patrick in tux vetting partiers at the door, chatting up cops, Wulftan wearing a red silk-lined cape and a wholly inappropriate red bow tie.

WXP sees a rich client even before having to recognize Patrick at the door. He habitually finds ways to avoid Patrick's level gaze. But Beryl lingers at the door. She carefully places her left hand on Patrick's heart and looks steadily into those eyes turned fey by horrors. She waits to feel his heart beat. Yes, it's beating faster. She nods, winks and goes in, as if attending to one last duty after having attended to her first duty to herself.

The Godling place strikes Wulftan as a roaring bay of pale boobs brushing an oily shoreline. Cleavages to baffle conversation. The men are the usual artifacts. He goes in, cops a decorative drink, being a teetotaler, and walks it out to the marble hallway to observe the party like a sailor in Hamburg's Reeperbahn peering into the red-lit windows of prostitutes.

Who wears an essential face, a face whose absence would leave a hole in the world? Is such a face an accident, the heroic, standard face of a patent fool, the incomparably beautiful face of a twit? Could such irony be random? Who is having the laugh here? It's enough to make one religious.

There's The Queen, tending bar, wearing a Roaring Twenties turban with a white feather pinned by a glass emerald brooch. Or is it glass? She has to be there, the affair can't be imagined without her. In fact, she's one of those necessary people who, once having been seen, seem to hold the earth in orbit. Who else is like that? Not Patrick, vetting people at the door. He's indispensable, but that's not the same as being necessary. Not the too elegant Jean-Luc. Not Beryl Sutphen, certainly not that boor of a husband who shouldn't even be thought of in the same breath. Not Wulftan Ertugay. Does Mr. Ertugay really know that about himself? Yes, I think he does. Not this Godling person, our host, God no. Any of these soignée golems in their evening clothes? Look, Jean-Luc, true to his innate flair, wears a white silk jacket, blue denims, and crimson sash, not a cummerbund but a sash. He hovers like a heron, catering to every whim, returning every smile, drawing out the most retiring, patting the shoulders of the jovial. The majordomo. The fix is in, and he knows it. He has always looked to Wulftan like a man who has just put in the fix. But he's not essential. When you come down to it, few people are. There's WXP huddling with fellow predators by an immense Palladian window as if he were imparting the one thing that will make them better vultures than they are. His type has to be somewhere, but not him, not specifically him. There's no specificity in him, he's interchangeable.

I prefer Sandinistas, Zapateros, Serbian ethno-creeps. In the end they do less damage than these consumers, but the damage they do is operatic and so it hands these creatures the means to distract the populace from pillage.

Now I will see why this Boudica, Grace Torrents, entrusted this galette with her story. Or will I. She will be here, surely, as Jean-Luc's doxy. How will he present her? Can she be imagined in an evening dress? Why not, there are vampires who dress their little girls like hookers and enter them in contests. Girls wobbly in heels incite some men, sadden others, worry some women, and make others weep.

He's looking into a gilt mirror in the hallway that leads to the gaily lit garden in the back when he sees Boo. Green is the holy light of Islam, the light one follows to enlightenment. Wulftan knows a great deal more than that about green. It's not a primary color, but it's a primary additive, a subtractive color. Considering the verdure of certain regions on the surface of the earth, it's hard to imagine its not being a primary color. Wulftan enters the mirror. Green-clad Boo is a bold brushstroke in the scene behind him in the grand reception room, a streak of green across the swashes and flashes of color. You could paint an ocean without green, you could paint an ocean without blue, but it would be gray or black, and that's what this party would be without Boo as Saint Elmo's Fire. Is this what she is to people: a flare, an elixir? But not an essential, not an elemental? If so, my life can be imagined without her, and I am just an old fart ogling the young'uns, as Patrick calls the girls in the park.

He looks up from his meditation, expecting his own sad face, but he sees Boo standing in the middle of that fabric-and-flesh conflagration looking straight at him. (Oh please, don't shoot me again.) He sees her move to her left to see his image in the mirror past his own shoulder. Then she's as still as a hawk in a dead tree. No finger is raised to shoot him. No one else seems to notice. Trey is approaching to his right. He will ask him if he's enjoying himself and Wulftan will answer, Yes, very much, so kind of you to invite me. And Trey will not invite him to meet the object of their conversations because he wants Wulftan to hunger. No one is manipulated without hunger. Trey is an amateur, Wulftan is not.

Before Trey reaches him, before Boo breaks her gaze, Wulftan slips away into a room on the other side of the hall and finds his way to the street. Patrick is still there.

I'll be back in a few minutes, Patrick. You'll remember me, won't you? The gaffer with the red tie?

I'll ask you for your papers, Wulftan. But if you don't have them, who will I turn you over to?

The authorities, Patrick. There are always authorities and they always have their hands out.

He walks west on 56th Street, holding his wolf's head cane like a rifle on his shoulder. Patrick has never seen him walk so briskly, like a janizary. He heads straight for the Korean grocer on Second Avenue and there he buys a single white tulip with some baby's breath. No, I don't want green tissue, he tells the grocer, I want white tissue. He's too good a customer for the man to show his annoyance.

***

Boudica isn't one to replay files of lost moments. She doesn't lose any, doesn't lose or forget anything. Trey's covetous gaze, his smirky little salutes to her with champagne flutes, break out like poison ivy on the insides of her thighs. This party isn't the moment, it's the flute into which moments have been poured. Jean-Luc winks at her, but is he sure? Sure she'll save his ass? And how would she do that? How would she let Trey Godling touch her in such a way that he thought it worth the bargain? How would he not taste barf in her mouth?

I've been to lots of parties, thanks to Slick over there. Slick knows the value of girlish legs in high heels. Oh yeah, I need Blind Hoxie in this hot mess, a few riffs from him and I'd know what to do. I need two dirty-water dogs. I need... to touch things—that bottle of Cristal Brut 1990 Methuselah, that goddam De Kooning I busted my toe getting in here, one of his dead women, that Russian sleigh chair, that Savonarola. I never wanted to come back here, to make a painting for this guy. There isn't a damned thing here that hasn't had the life sucked out of it.

***

The hands over her eyes are cool and smell of Clive Christian. Breathe deep, breathe slow, I know who you are, Boudica. Who am I?

Beryl. Beryl of the Beryl Isle.

Come sit in the garden with me, Boudica.

They watch the barges, tugs, pushboats, yachts, police launches. Roosevelt Island breathes on them in the thick air. Emerald-green Boudica, magnolia-white Beryl.

We're going to sit here and say nothing until everything is all right again, Boudica. Everything. I know your true profession and because of you I'm going to find my own, no matter how long it takes, and the hotshot there, all the hotshots, are incidental. They sit. Beryl doesn't know the deal, she can't know it. She can't know what Jean-Luc has asked of Boo. But she knows something.

Boudica is swathed rather than dressed in emerald green silk. Her gown whorls around her. Jean-Luc designed this rig, as he designed his own. Beryl runs her fingertips over Boo's face, she presses her eyebrows and smoothes them, she pinches the bridge of her nose, runs a forefinger across her lips. It's not lovemaking, it's a rearrangement of ether, of energy. Kid sister, mother, queen, nothing fits. Beryl and Boudica are bound like members of a landing party who have lost their memories. They know they can't get back to somewhere without each other. Whatever happens, they are members of the same party—and not this party.

***

Wulftan Ertugay's life has always depended on turning the moment inside out.

You have a permit for that? Patrick asked.

I am about to do your thing, Patrick.

He walks into the great room and stands just inside a Byzantine archway. The Queen spots him first. Always fast on the uptake, she lowers her head and points it towards Boo. Wulftan advances a few steps and stops. When Boo sees him he holds up the lonely tulip surrounded in baby's breath as a detective flashes a shield, not at a perp but at a witness. He holds it alongside his head and shakes it slightly.

All is revealed by the green light of Islam.

Boo knows what to do, about everything. She walks over to him and takes the tulip.

It's the only one you didn't put in my painting, Boo. All the other little upturned recognitions, their faces turned to heaven, are there. But you left this one out.

She pats his sides.

No, I didn't bring the Glock either, Boo. I have no one to shoot, and neither do you. I know who the muthafuckah is, and he doesn't need killing. You owe the muthafuckah a debt. He's quite an engineer. We have our faults. Did you really snip Eunuch Poe's figs?

Boo looks slowly around the room as if her head were a hand-held video camera. A debt. Can he possibly know what Jean-Luc wants her to do? Think fast, Boo. No, no, Wulftan doesn't know. He's referring to having met Jean-Luc. And as for Jean-Luc, he's talking to Beryl Sutphen. He salutes Boo with a champagne flute. All is well with his world, but Beryl knows it's not. She nods towards Boo and Wulftan, giving some kind of permission, some kind of permission she can't imagine but knows is needed. Everything is realigning here, everyone. Beryl feels slightly faint.

The consequence of being ourselves is awful, Wulftan says.

Boo knocks her head on his massive shoulder three times. He holds her away by her shoulders and sees tears wobbling in the corners of her eyes. He wipes a tear away with his finger and puts it in his mouth.

We'd do anything not to have to be ourselves. Why don't you and I face these consequences? The sonofabitch is dead. He's your sonofabitch, Boo, your personal, private sonofabitch.

A current berserks her upper lip, not a smile. She stares into his eyes.

Dead as he's ever going to be.

Dead as he's ever going to be, yes, Iceni queen, I believe that is so. Leave your faithful retainer here for now, leave Jean-Luc among the walking dead, where he belongs. We have work, you and I.

I want to tell him. Don't you want to know why he's the muthafuckah?

You want to tell him he's dead? Oh no, that would spoil it. He knows. He's always known. That's your attraction for him, that you're not, and like Boudica, never can be. I know why he's the muthafuckah. Come, let's go have our dirty-water dogs.